W9-CDL-379

SPACE
CAT-ASTROPHE

MY FANGTASTICALLY EVIL VAMPIRE PET

SPACE CAT-ASTROPHE

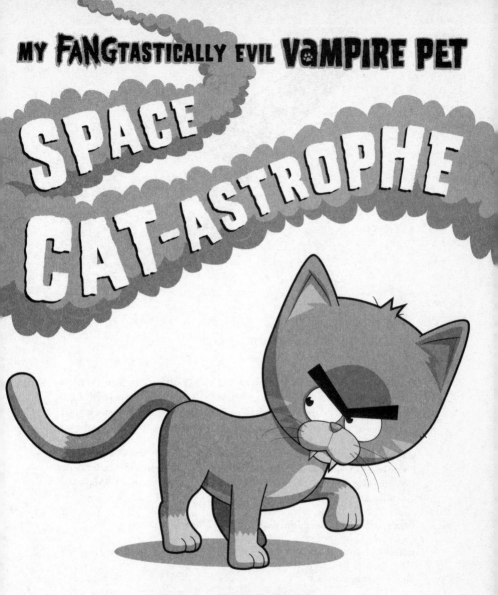

MO O'HARA

ILLUSTRATED BY MAREK JAGUCKI

FEIWEL AND FRIENDS ❧ NEW YORK

A Feiwel and Friends Book
An Imprint of Macmillan Publishing Group, LLC
175 Fifth Ave, New York, NY 10010

Space Cat-astrophe: My FANGtastically Evil Vampire Pet. Text copyright © 2019 by Mo O'Hara. Illustrations copyright © 2019 by Marek Jagucki. All rights reserved. Printed in the United States of America by LSC Communications, Harrisonburg, Virginia.

Our books may be purchased in bulk for promotional, educational, or business use. Please contact your local bookseller or the Macmillan Corporate and Premium Sales Department at (800) 221-7945 ext. 5442 or by e-mail at MacmillanSpecialMarkets@macmillan.com.

Library of Congress Cataloging-in-Publication Data is available.

ISBN 978-1-250-12813-3 (hardcover) / ISBN 978-1-250-12814-0 (ebook)

Book design by Carol Ly

Feiwel and Friends logo designed by Filomena Tuosto

First Edition, 2019

10 9 8 7 6 5 4 3 2 1

mackids.com

For my friends.

I write about friendship because
I have the best friends in the world.

SPACE CAT-ASTROPHE

This summer just got a little bit more epic. The camp counselors announced that our next challenge at Evil Scientist Summer Camp will be led by the totally awesome evil astronaut Neil Strongarm!! Yes, I said that right. Neil Strongarm. The Evil Astronaut, not the other guy. He is to astronauts what a triple-dip hot-fudge sundae with extra sprinkles is to plain old ice cream. Epic!

And I will actually get to meet him in real life! I've planned twenty-seven impressive things to say to him, come up with two cool new evil inventions, and even ironed my white evil-scientist coat. (As Neil says on page fifty-three of his autobiography, "You have only one chance to make an evil impression.")

Anyway, for one week Camp Mwhaaa-haa-ha-a-watha is turning into Evil Space Summer Camp. I am ready. Let the epic evil spaceness begin.

—The Great and Powerful Mark

1

"I just don't get it," Geeky Girl said for the third time.

"He's an astronaut and he's evil." I paused for her to take it in. "So he's an evil astronaut."

Geeky Girl's face looked like she was trying to figure out how to divide a really big number or something. Then she shook her head again. "He can't be both."

"Yes, he can," I said.

"Urgh," agreed Igor. Igor was a kid of few words. OK, no words, but he knew his stuff about evil celebrities.

Geeky Girl kept talking. "But how can a person spend time in the vastness of space and look back at the small, fragile blue marble—"

"Wait, they play marbles in space?" I interrupted.

"But that would be stupid 'cause, like, they wouldn't really roll, just float around—"

"I meant the Earth!" she interrupted back. "Because it looks like a blue marble from far away in space! How could someone look back on the fragile blue marble that is the Earth and not want to do something positive with their lives?"

I slumped down onto the bench. "Igor, show her the book."

The Man Who Should Have Been THE FIRST MAN ON THE MOON

Igor went over to one of the beds in the tent and picked up a hardback biography of Neil Strongarm. He handed it to Geeky Girl. "Urgh, urgh," he said.

She read the title, "*The Man Who Should Have Been the First Man on the Moon*," and then flipped it over to read the blurb on the back. "'One day, as I looked out of the spacecraft window back at the spinning blue marble in the vastness of space, I had a thought about my destiny.' See!" she said smugly, and then kept reading. "'I looked at the Earth, so tiny, and all the stars around it, and I thought, World domination is for wimps! I want it all! Space and everything!' Noooo . . ." Geeky Girl whimpered.

"I told you," I said. "Neil Strongarm is actually evil and he's actually an astronaut and he is actually coming here to camp to run the contest this week. This is gonna be so epic!!"

"Urgh, urgh, urgh," Igor added.

"Reeeooowl!" Fang jumped up on the book and clawed at the picture of Neil Strongarm on the cover.

"Hey, kitten, watch the book jacket." I scooped her up and put her on the bed next to Geeky Girl.

"I don't think Fang likes Neil Strongarm," Geeky Girl said.

"She hasn't even met him yet," I said. "And I can't exactly go up to him and introduce them, can I? Illegal pet in camp? Fang and I would be on the first canoe out of here."

"Urgh, urgh." Igor nodded his head.

BBBRRRRUUUUUUUUUUUUUMMMMMM!

Then the ground started to rumble. "Whhhooooaaaa," I said, grabbing the bench so I didn't fall off.

Fang dug her claws into the mattress and Geeky Girl's jeans to steady herself. "Owwwww, Fang!"

Geeky Girl unhooked Fang's claws from her now partly shredded jean leg. "What is that noise?"

"URGH!!!!" Igor shouted from the tent flap as he peered out. "Urgh, urgh!"

"He's here?!" I jumped off the bench and ran to the tent flap with Igor to look out.

"Who? And how do you know that's what Igor meant?" Geeky Girl said, standing up to join us.

"You spend long enough in a tent with a guy and you learn what his *urgh*s mean," I said. "It's Neil Strongarm's transport shuttle. It just landed."

Then the kid with the trumpet that gives us our evil wake-up call in the mornings started to play. There was a kid on the drums with him this time, though, too.

Dum . . . dum . . . dum . . . . DA DUM! the trumpet started. Then the drum kicked in. *Boom, boom boom boom boom boom boom boom boom boom.*

"Is that the movie theme from *2001: A Space Odyssey*?" Geeky Girl said.

"Yeah, he learned a new evil space tune in honor of Neil Strongarm," I said. "I would be worried that it might impress Neil, but really, when you spend time in small echoey spaceships, the last thing you want to hear is a lot of loud music."

Igor nodded again.

"So, did you come up with any plans to impress Neil Strongarm yet?" I asked Geeky Girl.

"I don't even think I want to impress an evil astronaut," she said, and shrugged.

"'Cause I've come up with some of my best evil inventions yet. I'm going to offer them to Neil, so he knows that I'm not just any old evil scientist kid. I'm an evil inventor too."

"So what have you got to show him that's so impressive?" she said, crossing her arms.

"OK, first, my Evil Super Space-Expanding Foam—*useful in all space station and spaceship scenarios. Everything from battle repairs to home improvements in space can be made easier with Evil Super Space-Expanding Foam*," I said in my best TV-commercial voice.

Igor clapped.

"Thanks, dude," I said.
"Oh, and Igor and I both
came up with the idea for the
Pogo Stick Lunar Travel
Individual Vehicle. *Useful
for low-gravity environments.
Cover more ground than
walking-jumping. Use less
energy. And have way more fun.*"

"A moon pogo stick?" Geeky
Girl said. "Yeah, you guys are
definitely going to impress him with that."

"Well, *you* haven't done anything," I said. "Look,
I know that you didn't want to be stuck in an evil
scientist summer camp, not actually being evil an'
all, but if you're here, you really gotta make more
of an effort." I paused. "Besides, I really like the
moon pogo stick thing."

"I told you, I don't care about impressing this
guy. You two go for the whole Evil-Emperor-of-
the-Week thing with whatever pretend space games
he comes up with. I'm not interested," she said.

Geeky Girl pulled back the tent flap and looked at the shuttle as it opened its hatch.

"Hey, do you think he'll show us the plans for his new evil space station, SSSH?" I asked Igor.

"Why do I have to *shhh*?" GG asked.

"You don't," I said.

"You just *shhh*ed me," she said.

"No, his space station that he's building. It's called SSSH—Secret Space Station Homebase. SSSH. Get it?" I said.

"*Sssh*-Urgh," Igor said.

"I get it," she said. "I just don't see what the big deal is about an evil astronaut." Geeky Girl shrugged her shoulders and strolled toward the landing site where all the campers had already started to gather.

Igor and I looked at each other, and then burst into a spontaneous high five. "Because it's the biggest deal ever!" I shouted.

"Urgh!" Igor squealed.

"But we gotta be chill, OK? You don't want to look desperate to impress him," I said.

"Urgh, urgh, urgh," Igor added.

"Totally, Igor. He'll definitely notice us—the best big, bald unibrowed dude and the coolest young evil scientist"—Fang clawed at my leg—"and that evil scientist's cat," I said as I scooped up Fang and put her inside my extra-deep kitten-size pocket on my white evil-scientist coat. We walked to the platform just as the stairs extended from the hatch and a big white astronaut boot stepped out.

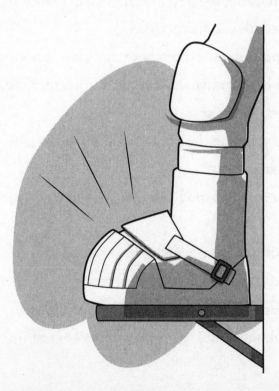

Trevor the Tech-in-ator's voice boomed out of the loudspeakers.

"Attention, please! The special guest for this veek's challenge has arrived."

Campers started to cheer and clap. There was a lot of happy mwhaaa-haa-haaing around the platform.

"Ve velcome the vonderful Evil Astronaut . . . Neil Armstrong!"

Igor and I gasped as a stony silence fell over the camp.

And then even worse, the astronaut boot stepped back into the shuttle craft.

There was the sound of a scuffle for the microphone and Trevor mumbling something

about "Vhy is he so sensitive anyvay?" Then
Phillipe Fortescue saying, "Just give her zee mic!"
Then the perky and enthusiastically evil voice
of Kirsty Katastrophe spoke. "The wonderful,
stupendous, best and most evil astronaut in the
world, who definitely was NASA's first choice to
walk on the moon and not that other guy whose
name no one can remember anyway"—she took a
breath—"we welcome . . . Neil Strongarm!!"

The white astronaut boot stepped out of the
shuttle again, this time followed by a man in a
white astronaut suit who stomped down the stairs
to the platform. "Amateurs," he mumbled.

While the camp counselors, Trevor, Kirsty and Phillipe, all came up on the platform with Neil Strongarm, shook his hand and led him to the microphone to speak to us all, I found myself just staring at him.

"I can't believe it's him. In real life. It's him," I said.

"Yes, you always liked him, didn't you?" I heard Sanj's voice over my shoulder. "Didn't you used to have a Neil Strongarm doll?"

"You had a Neil Strongarm doll?" Dustin repeated, flicking his super-bouncy hair off his super-clean-cut-looking smug face.

"It was an action figure. A licensed, limited-edition action figure!" I corrected.

"Anyway, I remember you playing with that doll"—he paused—"sorry, limited-edition action figure all the time," Sanj said. "It was sweet." He smiled and then laughed his evil wheeze. "But this is grown-up stuff now, Mark. Neil Strongarm is judging an evil space contest, not hanging out with superfans."

"You wait. Neil Strongarm will be hanging out with me, swapping evil plans, by tomorrow," I said, leaning into Sanj. Igor tapped me on the shoulder.

"Urgh?"

"*Us*, hanging out with *us*, I mean," I said.

"Hmmm." Dustin smirked. "Prepare yourself for disappointment."

Fang growled in my pocket, and I had to react super fast to block the paw swipe headed toward Dustin.

"You can't, kitten," I whispered to her as I held her down inside the pocket. "Remember, if they find you, we are outta here."

"AAAAAAchoo!" Bob sneezed as he walked past me. "I am definitely allergic to you, New Kid."

I kept holding Fang down in my pocket as I talked to Bob. If there was one person Fang would want to pounce on more than Dustin, it's him.

"Bob, you know my name. We share a tent. I've been here a couple weeks now. Can't you just call me Mark and stop with the New Kid thing?" I said.

Bob thought about it. "Nah. Bugging you by calling you New Kid is much more fun." Then he laughed a not-very-impressive "Mwhaa-haa-haa-haa" and pushed past us to join Diablo and the scary Goth-looking girl near the front of the crowd.

Neil Strongarm stood in front of the microphone now and tapped it with his finger. "Is this thing on? OK, so you know who I am. You should know who I am. I'm Neil Strongarm, the most famous evil astronaut that ever lived."

The crowd cheered.

"And I am the inventor and creator of the first evil space station, SSSH," he added.

The crowd went quiet again.

"Darn it, you don't have to shut up. I'm not *shhh*ing you. It's the name of the station. Secret Space Station Homebase. SSSH. You know, because it's secret." He paused. "Ah, never mind."

"Great name, sir," a wheezy voice spoke out from the crowd.

"Thanks, kid," Strongarm continued, and smiled down at Sanj in the front row. "But the real question is, why am I here talking to a bunch of kids in white coats?" Neil Strongarm leaned over the microphone.

"Because you are committed to empowering the next generation of evil scientists?" Dustin asked, flicking his hair as he spoke.

"No, of course not." He paused, glaring at Dustin. Then he looked over the mob of assembled campers. "Well, I'll tell you. Because a couple of you little, insignificant, unimportant, irrelevant nobodies might just get the privilege of becoming minions, I mean, apprentices on my space station."

A gasp came up from the crowd.

"I thought this was just going to be some stupid games about who could cope better in space or make the best stupid evil space plan or something. You are actually going to take one of us into space?" Geeky Girl spoke out from the crowd. "Did our parents sign a form about that?"

Trevor leaned into the microphone. "Yes, they signed the form," he said. "And technically Mr. Strongarm said he was looking for possible apprentices. So it could be more than one of you that goes into space."

"So he really could take a couple of us into actual space, then?" Geeky Girl's voice had gone up like she had sucked helium or something. "Into actual space?!!!"

Fang was now covering her ears, the pitch was so high, and Geeky Girl was bouncing on the spot, like Sanj's four-year-old sister, Sami, does when she knows it's time to watch *The Squeaky Piggy Show* on Cartoon Kid TV.

Neil took back the microphone and continued. "So you are all going to have to work hard to prove that you deserve to go into space with me. I'm going to test your stamina, your strength and your evil intelligence. Most of you will fail. But some of you won't, and the winning team will not only get to be Evil Emperor of the Week, but you'll also get the chance to be on my space team."

Now Igor was doing that excited bouncy thing that GG had been doing before. Only when Igor did it, he shook the ground. "Hey, man. Chill, Igor." I put a hand on his bouncy shoulder. "We got this; just play it cool."

As I looked over Igor's bouncing shoulder, I could see Trevor the Tech-in-ator, Kirsty Katastrophe and Phillipe Fortescue (the camp leaders) all bustling around the edge of the clearing surrounding the platform, setting up capsules on the outside.

Sanj noticed it too. "Dustin, what are they putting around the perimeter? It's like they are sectioning off this area beyond the tents. Curious."

Fang was getting suspicious of something too. She was making her uneasy growl from inside my pocket. Or maybe I was just imagining it. She'd heard Sanj's voice—that was enough to set off her Spidey Sense and make her think something was up.

"To make sure that I can accurately judge your performance in space, we have to create space-like conditions," Strongarm continued.

"Easier said than done," Sanj mumbled to Dustin.

"Easier said than done, you might think. But you would be wrong. With my invention, it's easy to create a space-like atmosphere. All you need to do is say, 'Release the space dome.'"

With that Trevor, Kirsty and Phillipe each pushed a button on the remote controls they were holding. All the capsules they had put around the perimeter burst and joined together as they inflated. In a matter of minutes, the whole area of the campground clearing was encased in this inflatable space dome.

Then I heard a *POP* and an inflatable tunnel shot out of the edge of the dome. Then another *POP!*, then another *POP!* Soon the dome was surrounded by connected tunnels that seemed to lead to other smaller inflatable areas.

This man was a genius. He'd invented a completely portable and easily inflatable space station.

"I know what you are thinking," Strongarm said at last, when all the *whoosh*ing of air from the inflating and the popping noises stopped. "You are thinking: This man is a genius. He has invented a completely portable and easily inflatable space station. And you would be right."

The crowd *ooooh*ed and applauded again.

"You are now in the prototype of SSSH."

The crowd went silent again.

"It's the NAME of the space station, people, remember?" Then he paused. "I might have to rethink this name. Anyway, you are in the prototype space station. And here is where you are going to train to be evil astronauts and where I am going to see who will survive."

3

I turned to Igor. "Did we just become the first kids ever to be encased in an inflatable evil space zone?" I said.

"Urgh!!" Igor bounced again and it made the whole dome shake.

"Result!!" We high-fived.

This was the best week at Evil Scientist Summer Camp yet. It was only a matter of time before Neil Strongarm realizes that he totally needed me with him in space. We were getting Evil Emperor of the Week and we were going into space! And the best part was that inside this dome there were no snakes or bears or even raccoons in a bad mood to ruin it. We were in a sealed environment now. It was down to us. Could we hack it in space or not? I say . . . bring on the space stuff.

All the kids were exploring inside the dome. Feeling the walls and looking into the tunnels.

Kirsty stepped up to the microphone. "Right, we are going to get ready for the first set of tests. We need to see how you respond to weightlessness and stress on the body under space conditions. We are adjusting the air pressure now. You will all start to feel the gravity changing here within the next few seconds."

As she said it, kids around me started floating up in the air and bumping into one another. Igor, not surprisingly, stayed on the ground the longest. And even in the zero gravity he just kind of floated low and hovered.

Geeky Girl pushed off from the ground and then started doing gymnastic flips in the air. She looked totally at ease in zero gravity. Neil Strongarm even noticed.

"Just ease into the feeling of weightlessness," he said. "Like that flippy girl over there. She's got the hang of it."

He'd now noticed Sanj and Geeky Girl, and he hadn't noticed me once. I had to do something that would make an impression on Strongarm. As I hovered in the air near him I hatched a plan.

He clomped over past me with his weighted space boots anchoring him to the ground. This was my chance. I mentally flipped through the list of impressive things I had come up with to say to him and randomly picked one.

"Hey, Mr. Strongarm, this is the most high-tech prototype space station I've ever seen."

He didn't even turn toward me. "You seen many of them, kid?" Neil Strongarm looked around at all the kids floating and flipping in the dome.

"No, I mean, but if I had, this would be way more advanced. Hey ... maybe we could chat evil plans sometime?" He walked by, not paying one bit of attention to what I was saying. He had that glazed look on his face that I get when English teachers start talking about irregular verbs. I had to act fast. I pulled out number seventeen from my mental list of things to say to impress Neil Strongarm. "Your ideas are so ahead of your time," I said, and then added in number twenty-three for good measure. "It's like you see the evil future and make it happen."

Neil Strongarm stopped and looked at me. "Yeah, that's pretty much what I do. Very perceptive. What's your name, kid?"

"I'm Mark . . ." I started to say when I noticed something floating just over Neil Strongarm's left shoulder.

It was the tail I saw first as it floated past, attached to a very surprised-looking kitten wearing a look that said, "This is totally against the laws of nature for me to be floating like this. What is happening?" She had her claws out and was rising quickly toward the roof  of the inflatable dome. I didn't know for sure, but I would guess that a scared, weightless kitten like Fang, trying to get out of wherever she was, could tear a hole in the dome in seconds and bring the whole thing deflating down on top of us.

I had to act fast. "Um, Mr. Strongarm . . . um . . . look over there. . . ." The first thing I saw in the other direction from Fang was Dustin spinning in the air and still managing to flick his hair, but it was like it was in a slow-motion space-hair commercial. "Look at that kid's hair!" I heard myself say, and pointed to Dustin.

"Wow, how does he get his hair to do that in zero gravity?" Neil mumbled.

Good. He was distracted.

I was hovering over Igor, so I leaned down and whispered, "Quick, throw me toward the roof."

"Urgh!" He launched me toward the roof and toward Fang. In midair I flipped, taking off my white evil-scientist coat with one move. Fang was all claws out and heading for the roof of the dome. I held out the white coat in front of me like a net. "I know you're not gonna like this, kitten," I whispered as I approached her. She had just turned and noticed me floating toward her with the outstretched coat and was about to let loose a very angry "Meeeooooow!" to protest this floating-around-a-dome thing that she was mad about. Time had run out. In one swift move I scooped up Fang inside the coat and balled it up under my arm. Phew.

And that's when Neil noticed me.

"Look!" Neil Strongarm pointed up at me. "That kid has got this Zero-G thing too."

He smiled and gave me a thumbs-up. Just at that moment, I crashed into the roof of the dome and bounced off. My speed increased because of the bounce and I headed right for Geeky Girl. I couldn't change my direction.

"What are you doing?" was the last thing I heard before I crashed right into her. All I remembered was her boot connecting with my head and the ball of evil-scientist coat holding the kitten slipping from my arms.

I woke up to a light slap in the face. I was back on the ground, and Kirsty Katastrophe was leaning over me. Everything in my body felt suddenly heavy, especially my eyelids. They drooped shut again. "Maybe I should hit him harder?" she said.

I opened my eyes. I heard an announcement saying, "Now that regular Earth gravity has been restored, please go change into your space suits, get your assignments and head to the appropriate section for testing."

"He's awake now," Kirsty Katastrophe said to Neil Strongarm, who was now leaning over me as well.

"Good agility, kid," Strongarm said. "Just watch where you're going. It's lucky for you that other kid grabbed on to something and pulled herself mostly out of the way."

I was groggy. My mind was slowly starting to put together what must have happened. I had been hurtling toward Geeky Girl, but she'd pulled herself up onto something, so I just connected with her boots. Then the next image came back to me. I was holding something. What happened to . . .

"My kitte—" I stopped myself. "My coat?!" I said out loud.

"What?" Neil Strongarm said. "You're not making sense, kid. Maybe he got hit on the head harder than we thought."

Then Geeky Girl leaned over me too. "Maybe you should stop talking and rest," she said. "You did bump your head pretty hard." She was holding my rolled-up white coat, and although she was covering it up pretty well, the coat was definitely wriggling. She gave me a look that said, *You are so lucky that I didn't rat you out.* "I'm going to go change into my space suit and leave my white coat in the laundry basket outside the changing room like we're supposed to," she said, and looked down at the wriggling coat.

"Yeah, right. I'm gonna, ummmm . . ." I started to say.

"Stop talking?" she said again. "And rest?"

"Yes, that," I said.

Kirsty Katastrophe took Neil Strongarm off to another section of the dome. I waited a second to sit up. My head was sore and I felt like I had been kicked in the head. Which was kinda true, except it was in reverse, because I'd head-butted a boot instead. I swung my feet around off the table and got up. Besides a bit of a headache, I felt OK.

Just outside the tunnel I came across Igor, Bob and Diablo, all being fitted for their space suits. Igor was still trying to zip his up.

"One, two, three, pull!!!" Trevor the Tech-in-ator was straining to inch up the final bit of the zipper. "Breavve in, Igor," he said, tugging on the zipper. Then with one giant suck-in of his stomach, Igor's zipper hit the top of the suit. "Phew." Trevor wiped his brow. "Right. Now for the challenges."

"Urgh, urgh, urgh," Igor gasped.

"Yeah, that looked like a challenge already, Big

Guy, but we gotta find out what the tests are for this space-race thing so we can ace them," I said.

"Are you done?" Trevor glared at me.

"Yeah, sure," I said.

"The first round of tests vill start right away vith the G-Force Simulator."

4

"The G-Force Simulator vill test your ability to vithstand the stress of takeoff and reentry on the mission. If you pass that, then you'll have to complete a Space Suit Strength Challenge." Trevor read off a sheet that had NASA SPACE SIMULATION TESTS written at the top of it. He looked around the room at the campers.

"Most of you von't make it past those stages. This is hard and there is no shame in failing." Then he stopped himself. "That is just a nice thing non-evil people say. Of course there is shame in failing. You vill have failed. Who writes this stuff? Anyvay, get on vith it and head to the area for the first test." People started to walk back down the tunnel.

Trevor stopped me. "You still need your suit," he said to me. "Quickly go collect it from outside the changing rooms. The assessments are about to start. If you're late, you lose."

"There's no way I'm losing," I answered, and ran off to collect my suit and change. I grabbed one off a rail of gleaming white suits and held it up to me to judge the size. "Yeah, this one should work," I mumbled to myself as I jumped into the outfit as fast as I could. I carefully stuffed some small evil space invention prototypes into my socks just in case I got to show them off to Neil Strongarm later. I was ready.

On my way out again, I caught my reflection in the mirror by the door. I had to take a second to look at myself in the suit. It looked good. I mean, I was born to wear a space suit, right? This was my destiny. The kid who shot his limited-edition licensed action figures into the sky on a plastic rocket was going to get to go into space. I just had to show them what I could do.

Oh yeah, and I had to find Fang.

Right, where was the laundry basket? Geeky Girl said she would put the coats in the laundry basket. I stopped at the one outside the boys changing room and searched through all the coats. Sanj came out of the room to put his in the basket while I was looking.

"Now, if I didn't know any better, I would swear that you look like someone who has lost their illegally smuggled and very sharp-clawed pet into a highly puncturable inflatable space station and is desperate to find it." Sanj smiled.

"No, I lost . . . ummm . . . my keys. Yes, I lost my keys, but I think I left them back in the tent, so no worries."

"Right, well, you better hope that you find her before I do, Mark. I'm not going to let an annoying little vampire kitten come between me and my career as an evil astronaut," Sanj said.

While he was talking, I saw something moving over by the girls changing room. Oddly, it was their laundry basket that seemed to be walking away on its own.

"Don't worry, Sanj," I said, still glancing at the moving basket out of the corner of my eye. "Fang won't need to ruin your chances, because you'll do that all by yourself. Now if you'll excuse me, I got a contest to win."

I walked off confidently in one direction until I was sure that Sanj had headed off in the other, far enough not to spot me doubling back to the changing rooms. I caught up to the walking laundry basket just as it was about to head down a tunnel leading to one of the assessment areas.

I flipped over the basket, and there was a very unhappy kitten.

"Not this way, Fang; we'll get caught." I scooped her up and went to tuck her inside my space suit but discovered the disadvantage of the cool-looking ultrafitted suit. There was no room to smuggle a cat.

So instead I tucked her under my arm and headed back to the changing room. As soon as we were inside she jumped down from my arm and started to meow at me. I don't speak cat, but she was basically telling me that she was mad. Very mad. And at me. I got that much.

"OK, Fang. I get that you didn't like the weightlessness and that you didn't want to be stuck in a laundry basket either." I stroked her behind her ear. "I'll find someplace to keep you safe, but for now I have to figure out how to get you to the next test without being spotted."

I looked at the list on the wall of the changing room. It was a timetable of who was in what test section and when. "I'm gonna be late!"

Trevor's words echoed in my head: "If you're late, you lose."

"I can't be late, because I can't lose, kitten," I said to Fang.

She growled at me.

"Sorry, I'm supposed to be in the G-Force Simulator pod now and then there's a Space Suit Strength Challenge."

Fang looked at me like that was not her problem. She jumped into a space helmet that was upturned on one of the benches in the changing room, curled up and tucked her head in to go to sleep.

"That's it!" I shouted, which made her pop her head over the top of the helmet.

"I can hide you in the helmet. I knew you were an evil genius, Fang," I said, and she purred.

I headed out of the changing room with the helmet tucked under my arm, cradling a curled-up Fang inside the lining. She was well-hidden.

Now all I had to do was get through the G-Force Simulator. How hard could it be?

When I got into the room I saw one of the simulators spinning to a halt on the turntable. The lid unlocked and the door slammed open wide. Dustin climbed out of the pod and went to flick his hair, but his normally perfect hair was now enormous and unflickable. The G-force had blown it all out so it was three times the size of his head. I already loved this thing if it did that to Dustin's hair.

He touched his newly expanded hairdo. "Argh! My hair?! Someone get me a mirror! This is a hair emergency!"

"I don't think they have hair emergencies in space." Geeky Girl smiled at Dustin as she walked off to the next station.

I guess Geeky Girl had already done the
G-Force Simulator and gotten through. Igor
looked like he was waiting for his turn.

"That ride looks like fun. I'm next, right?" I
climbed in and handed my helmet to Igor. "Can
you look after this for me, dude? It's very delicate,
so be careful," I said, tilting the helmet to show
Igor what was inside.

"Urgh, urgh!" he said.

I jumped into the
pod like it was a sports
car and I was in a TV
show about a guy who
drove sports cars. (Or
maybe a guy who drove
sports cars and then went into
space. Yeah, that.) They strapped me into the chair
and closed the hatch. Suddenly it felt less like
riding in a sports car and more like being encased
in a giant washing machine. It was noisy and I
couldn't shake the feeling that I was just about to
be put onto a megaspin cycle.

A voice came through the speaker inside the pod. It was Phillipe. "In zis test, zee machine will simulate a portion of zee G-force zat you would face on a descent back into Earth's atmosphere. If you don't pass out, we take zat as a pass." He made a smug little laugh to himself. "Zee test will start now."

I could feel the machine begin to move, then get faster and faster and faster. This pod thing whipping around on a giant arm was faster than any roller coaster or fairground ride I'd ever ridden. I started to feel sick, but then I started to feel something even weirder. My skin was moving. It was being forced back, making wrinkles that must have looked like a pug dog's face. How is that even possible?

But more important, what if it stayed like that? What if I became a famous astronaut, but I did it with the face of a wrinkly dog? I guess it wouldn't be all bad. I'd get a lot of publicity as an astronaut with a pug face. The speed was building to a peak. Then, just as I was imagining all my mega-promotion TV deals for being a famous dog-faced astronaut, the spinning started to slow down. By the time it stopped, I could move my hands, and I reached up to touch my face. Back to normal. Well, no TV deal, but at least I still looked good.

Someone unlatched the door to the pod but hadn't opened it yet to unstrap me from my seat.

I could hear the kids getting ready for the other G-Force Simulator and some of them heading over to the Space Suit Strength Challenge across the hall.

I could hear Dustin saying, "That helmet is way too small for me now that my hair is this big. I'll need to use the big kid's helmet for the challenge."

"Very well. Igor, give zee helmet to Dustin for his challenge, and zen you can have it back when it's your turn," Phillipe said.

"Urgh, urgh, urgh, urgh!" Igor protested.

"Now, or you give up your chance, Igor," Phillipe insisted.

"No!!" I shouted from the pod, but no one listened.

I could hear footsteps as Dustin walked away to start the Space Suit Strength Challenge.

"Let me out! Someone unstrap me! Come on! I want to do the next thing!!!" I shouted.

Phillipe eventually came up and unstrapped me. "Very impressive," he said. "You passed."

"Thanks, but I've got to get to the strength challenge!"

Phillipe nodded. "Igor, you're next. Climb in."

I jumped down from the simulator and Igor pointed to Dustin, who had just put on my helmet and was starting the challenge. I was too late.

"Urgh, urgh, urgh." Igor patted my shoulder as he got into the pod. The arm of the machine creaked from the weight.

I ran over to the Strength Challenge Zone and looked. Any minute now Dustin would say, "There's an illegal pet in my helmet," and rat me out. Or cat me out.

I waited.

Dustin was in the suit and helmet and attached to a weighted harness. He had to perform certain lifting and walking tasks to see if he was strong enough to do them in increased gravity.

Suddenly Dustin started flailing his arms and hitting his helmet with his gloved hand. You couldn't hear what he was saying in the helmet, but he was motioning to get the helmet off. He couldn't do it himself. He was panicking.

Trevor came over and unhooked the helmet and lifted it off Dustin's head.

This was it. I had passed the first test, but my space race was stopping here and Fang and I would be sent home from camp in the Canoe of Shame.

Trevor dropped the helmet to the floor. No kitten rolled out of it.

Dustin was still shaking. "There was something in the helmet! Something was in there!!!" he shouted.

Trevor looked inside. It was empty. "There is nothing there. You vere experiencing space claustrophobia from being inside the helmet."

Then I saw a bit of Dustin's hair move. Fang? Was she hiding in the hugeness of Dustin's hair?

6

I ran up to Dustin, taking off one of my big space-suit gloves as I did. "Hey, bad luck, Dustin," I said as I patted his hair, scooping Fang into the big glove at the same time.

"Watch the hair, man." Dustin twitched away. "There was something in that helmet. Something humming, purring. A little voice."

Trevor led him away down one of the tunnels. "This means you vill join the others who didn't pass the challenges so far." On the way out, though, Dustin stopped for a second to say something to Sanj. I couldn't hear what they were saying, but Dustin leaned in and whispered to Sanj. Then they did one of those handshakes that I've seen my dad do in restaurants. You know, where he slips the waiter five bucks in the handshake. Well, I don't think Dustin was giving Sanj five bucks, but I'm sure he passed him something. I thought about investigating, but I was too far away to see what it was, and anyway, I didn't have time to think about little stuff like that. I had a contest to win.

"Right," Kirsty said, handing me the helmet from the floor. "Your challenge starts in ten seconds. Move those blocks to the other side of the room. Easy, right?"

There was no time to ditch Fang. I quickly dumped her from the glove into the helmet as I swung it up to put it on my head. I could hear her well-known I'm-so-mad-at-you hiss as I clicked it into place and put down the visor. Kirsty helped me with my gloves and then tapped my helmet.

"Starting . . . now!" she shouted.

Fang was trying to balance herself inside my helmet as I moved forward in the space suit. Moving was weird. It was like when the gravity in the dome was turned down and we were weightless, but I was in this heavy spacesuit and helmet. It felt hard even controlling my arms and legs now that I was strapped in. I took a step and bounced in the wrong direction. Fang dug her claws into my head to steady herself.

"Owwwwwh! Kitten!" I shouted inside the helmet.

"You OK? You're not making sense again." Kirsty Katastrophe's voice came through my earphone in the helmet. I forgot that this helmet had a mic! "Are you having delayed reaction to that head slam with the girl's boot?"

"No, I mean, you must be kidding? Starting already?" I said, trying to shake my head to make Fang undig her claws from my scalp. "I'm OK. I got this."

"You better. You only have three minutes to complete the task—or you fail," Kirsty said.

"I can't fail. I will do this," I said to myself and to Fang and Kirsty.

"Yeah, whatever," she answered. "Two minutes, fifty seconds."

I blinked my eyes and got my bearings. I picked up the first box and started moving, but I was bouncing around again. Then I could feel Fang relax her claws and curl up inside the helmet. She started to purr. Guess she found a comfy spot.

"What's that sound?" Kirsty asked.

"Ummmmm, it's a ummmm . . . meditation technique," I said. "Yeah, it helps me concentrate."

Weirdly, Fang's purring did calm me down. *I can do this*, I repeated to myself, but in my own head this time, not through the microphone.

I got the first box to its place and headed back for the second. With each step, I felt more in control.

I picked up the second box and took bigger jumps to get back down to the other end of the room. I did it in half the time.

"See," I said, "I got this moon-walking thing. No problem."

I had thirty seconds on the clock and one more box to move. I bent down to pick up the final box when it happened. A sleeping kitten slipped off the top of my head and slid right down the visor to block my view. All I could see was gray fur. Suddenly the purring was not so relaxing.

I grabbed the box and started to move, but I had no idea where I was. I could be heading the wrong way! I tried wiggling my nose and even poking Fang with my tongue to get her to wake up, but nothing worked. I just got a very furry tongue!

"Bleh!!!" I spat out cat fur.

"You've got ten seconds. What's the problem?"
Kirsty said.

I had to get Fang out of my face so I could
see, but I couldn't just knock her out of the way.
Or could I? I jumped up into the air as hard as I
could, and then rolled forward in a tuck, holding
the box. As I came out of the turn in the air, Fang
slid back off my face and I could see where I was. I
hit the ground again and bounced hard toward the
end of the room. My boots touched the ground,
and I put the box on the pile as the clocked ticked
to zero.

I could see Igor through my fur-covered visor.
He was mouthing "Urgh! Urgh! Urgh!" and was
clapping.

Kirsty's voice came over the helmet speaker.
"OK, that's a pass. You can head over to the next
station for the flight-simulation test."

I kept my helmet on while they unstrapped me
from the harness. Geeky Girl was up next.

I gave her a thumbs-up as she got clipped in.

She smiled through the visor of her helmet, and then pointed to mine. A tip of gray tail was just sticking out of the corner.

I quickly tucked it back in, turned and headed off to the changing rooms.

When I got inside, I took off the helmet and out rolled Fang onto the bench. She was still snoozing!

"Fang! Time to wake up," I said, wiping all the fur out of the inside of the helmet with some paper towels. "We have one more contest to get through for this phase. It's the flight simulator, and I can't take a chance on you messing this up."

Fang didn't even blink. She was out for the count.

"So, I'm going to just leave you here for a bit. You'll be OK, right?" I said, piling towels around her to hide her. "Don't move and don't leave the changing room, all right?"

Fang made a sleepy purr and rolled over.

I tiptoed out of the changing room so I wouldn't wake her and then bolted to the next station. As I got to the flight simulator, though, I heard *ooohs* and *wows* coming from a small group of kids that had formed around the simulator pod. Whoever was in there was acing this flight. The stats on the screen were incredible. Speed, agility, precision. Those were all the rankings, and whoever it was was getting top marks in everything. Then I saw the name on the board: Sanj!!!

This was impossible. Sanj sucked at video games. He always lost in the battlefield games, and in space games, he usually got a little dizzy from spinning at warp speed and crashed a couple minutes into the game.

But the stats on the screen told a different story. Sanj didn't make one wrong turn. He steered perfectly and docked at the virtual space station in record time. Sanj was king of the flight simulator. He was a racing demon. A speed-flying legend. He might even be good enough to be Evil Emperor of the Week or, worse, to get Neil to take him into space!

7

This was not real. I must have accidentally transported to some bizarro world where Sanj was good at video games! Where was I? He had to have rigged it somehow. I'd played games with him for years and he'd never not crashed out in a burning fireball. Something was not right.

"That vas excellent," Trevor the Tech-in-ator said as Sanj got out of the pod.

"Yes, I did think it would be more challenging, but you know." Then he paused and touched his ear. "Thank you," he added, and did one of his trademark *mwhaa-haa-haa* wheezes.

Diablo was just finishing on the other machine. "You need more speed on that thing, man," he said, tossing his helmet to Bob as he jumped out of the pod. "And blasters. You need more blasters!"

"You are just flying up to and docking vith the space station. You are not supposed to blast it," Trevor said.

"Oh, my bad," Diablo said.

"You passed anyvay," Trevor added. "You docked the ship perfectly before you blasted it, so technically you passed."

OK, note to self. Don't blast the space station until after you dock.

"Result!" Diablo high-fived with Bob as they crossed over to look at the results on the screen. They were both through, and now Sanj was through as well. I thought more of the competition would drop away with each test. Never mind, I still had this. The flying simulator was my ace in the hole. I was great at this kind of thing, and if Sanj could do it, then they were right, this would be easy.

I strapped in and closed the hatch on my simulator pod.

"Right, the vheezing kid had a good point. Too many people are passing this test, so it must be too easy. This time ve'll reset so the simulation pods are racing each other."

"Wait, so only one of us gets to go through?" I said.

"That's vhat I said," Trevor spoke down the mic. "Are you strapped in and ready?"

"All ready to win this race and head to space," I said, smirking.

Then I heard the other voice on the headset. The voice from the other pod.

"I'm ready," Geeky Girl said. "No hard feelings, Mark, but I am going to win."

"It's you? I'm racing you?" I started to say, but Trevor spoke over us.

"Whoever gets to the space station first and docks vins, and that person, and that person only,

vill go through from this round. Ready and go."
As Trevor stopped talking, a buzzer sounded and
then the pod started shaking like it was simulating
a takeoff.

I was racing Geeky Girl to get to the virtual
space station and only one of us could win.

I pushed on the thrusters and engaged the
turbo-drive engines. I maneuvered in front of
Geeky Girl right away and held my position,
blocking every time she tried to pass. All those
months of *Battle Planets X* that Mom said were
a waste of time were now saving my chances of
actually going into space. I had this.

I could see the space station on my trajectory. I
would definitely get there first. Geeky Girl would
have to walk down that inflatable corridor with
the other losers. I felt kinda bad for her. She would
make a good astronaut, but that was the problem.
She would make a "good" astronaut, and what Neil
Strongarm needed were "evil" astronauts. She just
didn't have it in her. She couldn't survive in the
cutthroat competition of space.

I was the best evil astronaut, and now Neil Strongarm would see that. I would be one step closer to being crowned Evil Emperor of the Week and, most important, being picked by Neil and going into space. I was just picturing how I could get a crown welded onto a space helmet when it happened.

Geeky Girl blasted me. The pod shook as my left engine light flickered. She shot me in my left booster!! But this was a race, not a battle.

I engaged the communications link between the pods. "What are you doing, Geeky Girl?"

"Winning" was the reply that came back. "It's every person for themselves. Sorry, Mark, I have to do this. I have to get into space."

My virtual ship spluttered and slowed, and Geeky Girl pulled into the lead. I looked out my hatch window from the pod and saw that the whole group of campers had stopped to watch Geeky Girl and me race. We were not just doing this in a virtual world on-screen, we were doing this in front of the whole camp.

OK, if this is how she was going to play this, then I had step up my plan. But first I had to stop the power drain. It was time for my secret weapon. I took my flash drive with the virtual program for the Evil Super Space-Expanding Foam out of my sock and plugged it into the simulator control panel. OK, now to deploy the expanding space-foam hole plugger to stop up the blast hole in the left booster. Done.

Then I looked at the control panel in my pod and imagined I was playing *Battle Planets X*. What would Captain Titan do in the game? He would probably sacrifice himself to save his shipmates and the mission. No way was I going to do that. First, I had no shipmates in this simulation, and second, there was no way I was giving up on this that easily. Then I thought, What would Neil Strongarm do?

I smiled as I diverted power from the landing gear, the communications systems, the navigation systems and the life-support systems. The left booster surged back into action with the diverted power.

Trevor's voice came over the speaker in my helmet. "You are not allowed to override the simulation like that."

I ignored him. I had to catch up to Geeky Girl. I was flying by sight without the tracking systems and speeding along as fast as the rockets would take me. She was seconds away from docking, but I was gaining on her.

I started to feel light-headed. Oh yeah, the oxygen level was dropping in the pod.

"If the oxygen level falls below the next level, I'm stopping the simulation," Trevor said.

Then I heard another voice—one that I recognized. "No, let him do it." It was Neil Strongarm.

I was right on Geeky Girl's tail now. I was about to pass her when she jettisoned her back rockets into my path. I had to swerve hard right to avoid them.

Geeky Girl had lined up her ship perfectly with the docking station. Even without her rockets, the momentum pushed her into position.

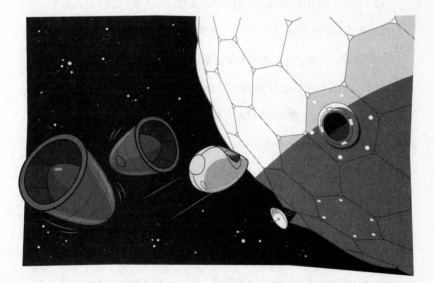

"Noooo!" I shouted as I was spinning off to the right, still reeling from my quick swerve.

Geeky Girl was seconds away from docking. She was going to win this.

Then I heard the voice again. "Shame, I thought that kid had something." It was Neil Strongarm again.

I hated the sound of disappointment in his voice. I would not lose this. Not even now. What would Neil Strongarm do?

Then it occurred to me—if the docking port at the space station was blocked then I would have to make a new one ... by blasting a new hole in the space station and docking there.

I fired up the blasters and shot. The laser cut through the walls of the virtual space station, making a hole just big enough to land. I spun the ship around and reverse-parked into the hole in the station. I could see Geeky Girl complete her docking as I deployed the expanding space-foam hole plugger to seal the hole up behind me. I popped the hatch to my pod just before I passed out from low oxygen. I remember Trevor and Igor lifting me out of the simulation pod and leaning me against the base as

I took deep breaths. The next thing I knew Neil
Strongarm was standing over me.

"I like the way you think, kid. If you don't
like the rules, then change the rules." He smiled.
"Sometimes that works."

"Both of these kids pass," he said to Trevor.

"Right. All of you who have gotten this far vill be put into teams for the next assessment. The rest of you"—Trevor pointed down the long inflatable corridor—"that is the vay out!"

8

Most of the other campers walked down that corridor. Some of them had to be carried by Phillipe because they wouldn't accept that they had lost.

There were only a dozen of us left now, and Kirsty stood in front of us all with a clipboard, pacing back and forth.

"You kids have made the first cut." She smiled, but then she scowled. "But ONLY the first cut.

The next assessment is to test how well you work in teams and how fast you can think."

"There's no time in space for dillydallying," Neil interrupted. "You have to think and then act."

Then Kirsty read out the teams.

The trumpet kid, the drum kid and a scary Goth girl were on one team.

Three really scared-looking nerdy kids were on another team.

Sanj, Bob and Diablo were on another.

And then she read out my team.

"Mark, Igor and Geeky Girl."

"Great, so I have to work with the girl who literally just shot me in the back?" I said.

"Or you could give up now?" Kirsty said.

"Fine," I said.

Igor patted me on the back. We would have to make this work. At least we had a team that had Igor's strength and Geeky Girl's techy knowledge and my general evil greatness. We could ace this challenge. If Geeky Girl didn't double-cross us to win.

"Go into your allocated rooms, and you can start your test," Kirsty said.

I high-fived Igor as we headed to the room. Geeky Girl followed. She had taken off her helmet and was holding it by her side. Under the visor, I spotted a wing flutter slightly. She lowered the visor gently to cover up the budgie inside. So that's where Boris has been this whole time. Then I remembered. Fang! She was still in the changing room!

"Ummm, I have to go to the bathroom," I blurted out. "All that lack-of-oxygen thing really made me . . . ya know . . . need to go," I lied.

Kirsty rolled her eyes. "You have two minutes to get to your rooms. Once the door is closed, the clock starts and the door won't reopen until the assessment is over. If you're out when the door closes, you fail." She paused. "And your team fails."

Geeky Girl and Igor gave me a look that said, "You better make it back." I ran to the changing room and rifled through the towels, looking for Fang. The clock was ticking. Where was she?

Then I heard her. "Meeeeeoooowww!"

Fang was balancing on the door top, ready to pounce. "Good attack cat," I said, "but we have to go."

Fang jumped down. "So how am I going to sneak you into the room without anyone seeing?"

Fang curled up on the floor like she didn't care.

"You can't sleep more. Come on, we have to leg it," I said.

"That's it. Leg it."
I pulled up my flight
suit pants leg and she
climbed up and clung
to my sock. Then I ran.

I made it to the
door just as it started
to beep and close.
I dove through and
skidded across the
floor as it clicked shut.
Phew.

"Cutting it close,"
Geeky Girl said.

"So? What are you gonna
do about it?" I said back. "Blast me?" I paused. "Oh
yeah. You did."

"I VIRTUALLY blasted you, Mark, in a
simulation. We both want to win, and we are both
willing to play hard to do it," she said.

"So what happened to the you-two-go-for-
the-Evil-Emperor-of-the-Week thing? I'm not

interested." I did my best Geeky Girl impersonation as I threw her own words back at her.

"We're not fighting for some stupid crown now. We are fighting to go into space, and I really, really, really want that," she said.

"OK, first, crowns aren't stupid," I said.

Igor grunted to agree.

"And second, we all want that."

"Then it's good we're on the same team this time then, isn't it?" Geeky Girl said, and cracked a smile.

"OK, we'll do this together. And look. I just brought in our secret weapon," I said as I rolled up my pants leg and Fang jumped down. Instantly Boris flew out of the helmet and the two animals faced off.

"We don't have time for this now," Geeky Girl told off Fang and Boris. "We find out what the challenge is and we'll only have half an hour to complete it or we fail." She looked Fang right in her big green eyes. "And I'm going into space!" Fang stared hard for a moment, then swished her tail at Boris and started to wash her paws like that was her intention all along, not to start an epic budgie battle at all.

I looked around. "Hey, maybe we should keep the pets hidden anyway, just in case there are cameras in here."

"I already did a sweep before I let Boris fly out," Geeky Girl said. "I brought some basic bug-sweeping devices with me in my backpack. You never know when you'll need to know if you're being watched."

"You are really paranoid, but it works," I said.

Phillipe's voice came over the loudspeaker in the room. "Welcome to your team challenge. Your task for zee next thirty minutes is to create a method of propulsion for a space vessel using only zee materials zat you find in this room."

There was a sheet covering a bunch of items on a large table in front of us. Igor pulled back the sheet and threw it on the floor. There were fans, engine parts, motor parts, cogs, wheels, all kinds of things, and some tools.

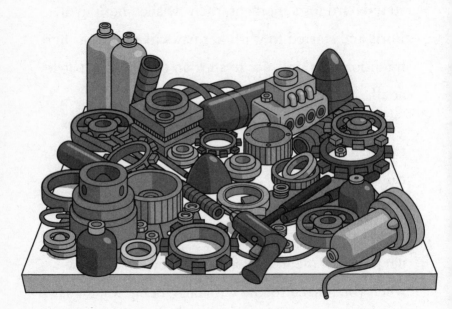

"So we need to make a rocket or a booster or something to power a spaceship," I said.

"It has to be a method of propulsion, so something that moves a ship through space," Geeky Girl said.

"Is there anything that you could use to make a moon pogo stick?" I asked.

Igor shook his head, then he picked up some engine parts and started putting them together.

"That would work great, Igor," Geeky Girl said, "but we don't have any fuel to run an engine."

"OK, let's think. What else can we use for power?"

"Electricity?" I said. Then I looked around the room and saw that there were no plug sockets and no batteries either.

"OK, what about hydropower?" Geeky Girl said.

"No water," I answered.

Then Igor picked up a fan and started blowing on it. "Urgh?"

"Wind power is a good idea, but I don't think we have enough to power a rocket," I said.

"But Igor might be on the right track. I saw this NASA program about solar sails being used in space. The solar winds push the sails. Maybe we could make something like that?" Geeky Girl said.

"Shame we don't have anything on the table to make a sail," I said.

Then Igor picked up the sheet that had been covering the stuff from the table off the floor. "Urgh?"

"OK, but we can't just wait for a solar wind to push us. There isn't any in here. So we have to have something more dynamic," Geeky Girl said.

"You want it to be a more exciting sail, then paint a big super sail logo on it or something, but I don't think that will help," I said.

"I mean it has to do more on its own. It can't be pushed by something. It has to actively move," Geeky Girl said.

We spent the next twenty minutes or so building two sails and engineering them to pivot and move with all the stuff from the table.

"It still won't move on its own, though," I said, and sat down next to Fang. But I accidentally sat on her tail, which caused her to jump up and land right by the helmet that Boris was nesting in. Boris flapped up into the air but caught the helmet strap with her leg as she took off. The helmet then slammed into my head as she flew up to get out of Fang's reach, and that's when Geeky Girl shouted, "Eureka!" at the same time I shouted, "Owwwwwwwch!"

She was doing that bouncing thing again like before. "Wings!!!"

9

"We need dynamic solar WINGS, not just sails," Geeky Girl said. "The wings will give enough uplift to continue the momentum in space, and they will be powerful enough to carry something too."

"Like Boris carrying the helmet!" I said.

"Urgh!!" said Igor.

We looked at the clock. Five minutes.

We dove into the pile of stuff and came up with anything we could use to attach the sails (which we bent and folded to look like Boris's wings) to a pod that we constructed around the helmet. When the mechanism was wound up, the wings would flap and the helmet would be lifted off the ground. We bolted and screwed everything into place just as the buzzer sounded and the door opened.

No time to test it. We just had to cross our fingers and hope for the best.

All the kids came out of their rooms. Fang climbed back up my pants leg and Boris fluttered back into the helmet to hide.

We walked out with Igor gently holding our Dynamic Solar Wing, whatever it was.

Sanj, Bob and Diablo strode out of their room with a very neat motorized handheld rocket.

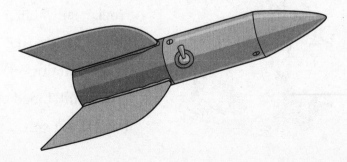

The trumpet kid and the drum kid came out of their room looking scared. They carried a pile of stuff that looked vaguely like a rocket, but it also looked like it had already fallen apart several times. They were followed by the Goth girl, who just looked really, really mad.

And the other team of young evil scientists came out with lots of space junk taped onto one kid on their team. They called it a "motor robot rocket suit," but it just looked like a kid with lots of space junk taped to his flight suit.

As we were getting ready to show our stuff to Trevor, Geeky Girl leaned over and whispered, "You know how I had some sweeping equipment to pick up bugs?" I nodded. "Well. I'm picking up a sound device coming from Sanj."

I looked over at Sanj. He was adjusting something on his ear. Just like he did back in the flight simulator. "I thought that Dustin gave him something when he left," I whispered back to Geeky Girl. "I think he must have given Sanj a secret speaker that he's using to communicate with Sanj from the outside. There's no way Sanj could have flown like that on his own."

"Dustin could be helping him?" Geeky Girl said. "We have to tell on him. Then they'll be disqualified, and we'll be closer to getting into space," she said, and started to walk toward Trevor.

"Not so fast." I stopped her. "If they know Sanj has been cheating, then they'll search us all just to be sure, and they'll find a certain budgie and kitten."

She huffed, "You're right. So we have to let them get away with it?"

"For now," I said. "We just have to get to the next assessment. We can do this. We make a good team. Maybe Neil will see that and send all three of us on the mission to SSSH."

"Vhy are you *shhh*ing me? I vasn't saying anything," Trevor shouted at us. "Right, let's see how you did."

Trevor the Tech-in-ator walked down the line of kids, looking at all our projects. "Phillipe vas supposed to judge this assessment as vell, but he must have had to step out during the challenge."

He went up to Sanj's team first.

"Can you demonstrate how this vorks?" Trevor said.

"Sure," Bob said, and then looked at Diablo.

"Yeah," Diablo said, and then looked at Sanj.

"Of course." Sanj smiled smugly. "All you have to do is flick the switch here and the onboard kinetic motion motor powers up. It requires exactly thirty seconds to achieve maximum RPM before you simply launch the hand rocket manually from an elevated surface." He paused.

"You throw it from
a height." He paused
again and looked over at
Igor. Sanj walked up to
Igor, and said, "May I?"

"Urgh." Igor nodded.

Sanj then climbed up,
stood on Igor's shoulders,
and threw the rocket up.
It whizzed around the room
for a few minutes, and we
all had to duck for cover
until it ran out of power.

Sanj looked over at
Trevor once the rocket
was safely on the ground.
"So, is that a pass then?"

Trevor nodded and
moved on to the motor
robot rocket suit next.
"You can begin your
demonstration," he said.

The three kids on the team all looked at one another and nodded. The smallest of the kids was wearing this robot stuff, including a silver helmet. He had panels with buttons and screens on his chest and what looked like big hair dryers on his feet. He took a deep breath, and the other kids flicked some switches and turned some dials on the suit. First, it started to make a noise like you would expect giant hair dryers attached to someone's feet to make. Then it started to make a noise like giant hair dryers attached to someone's feet would make . . . if they were about to explode.

The kid in the suit started shaking and shouted, "Turn it off!!!" right before the hair dryers shot him up into the ceiling. Lucky for him we were in an inflatable dome, so he just bounced off. The kids and Trevor had to tackle him and turn the hair dryers off.

"Fail!" Trevor said, and walked on to the trumpet kid's team.

"So, we made a power pack powered by the reverberation of sound from our instruments," the trumpet kid started to say.

Their project looked like what would happen if you put a trumpet, a drum kit and a bicycle into a transporter and pressed "mix," and even worse, it looked like it was being held together with . . . well, with nothing, really. As soon as they started talking, bits started slowing falling off the rocket.

"Yeah, but the problem was that the same sound waves that made the ship move also shook it apart like a little drumming, trumpeting earthquake!" the Goth girl said, stomping her foot and sending a pile of spaceship debris crashing to the floor.

"Fail again!" said Trevor, walking past them. Then he looked at us. "This better be good."

"We have made a really cool and totally original 'Dynamo wing solar thing,'" I said. As I spoke Fang was still clinging to my tube sock on my leg. I could feel her wriggling under the leg of the space suit. When she got fidgety that usually meant one thing and one thing only. Scratching.

Geeky Girl stepped in front of me with Igor holding the machine. "I call it a 'Winged Onboard Oscillating Solar Sail Hybrid' or 'WOOSSH' for short. Names are very important, you know."

I tried to casually readjust my sock while Geeky Girl spoke.

Neil Strongarm walked down the corridor at that moment. "I agree. Names are so important," he said. "But does it work?"

Igor wound up the mechanism, and we set it on the ground. Geeky Girl adjusted the wings, and then stepped back. "You see, in Earth's gravity it will fly, but in the vacuum of space the momentum of the wings will carry the ship much farther than a fossil-fuel explosion could. It should be a more economic and environmentally friendly way to travel in space," she started to say until I elbowed her in the ribs. "But obviously that is just an accidental side effect, because I wouldn't care about that, because I am of course ... evil." She smiled at Neil Strongarm, and did a pretty passable "Mwhaa-haa-haa-haa." Then she flipped the on switch and the WOOSSH began to wobble, then flap, and then it took off. It worked!!! I think we were just as surprised as Neil Strongarm.

It took Igor and me a couple minutes to catch the thing and turn it off. All the while, Fang's claws had sheared through my sock, and she was digging into my leg to hang on. My teeth clenched and I tried to breathe through the pain. After we caught the WOOSSH, Trevor spoke to us.

"So, two teams go through and two teams have failed. You know vhere to go now."

The losing teams headed down the corridor Neil Strongarm had just come from. It was only six of us now.

"I'm mixing up your teams again," Trevor said. "Diablo, you are vith Geeky Girl. Bob, you are vith Igor, and Mark, you are vith . . ."

"Sanj?" I said, and slumped down onto the floor by some boxes. At the mention of Sanj's name, Fang slid down and crawled out of my pants leg. She ducked behind one of the boxes and glared across the room at Sanj.

10

Neil Strongarm spoke up. "You might be working with people you don't like. You might be working with people you don't trust. Good. You'll be in space someday soon—if you're lucky—and you'll have no one to rely on but yourselves. Be your own team. There is no *I* in *team*, and there is no *I* in *space travel*, but there is an *I* in *survival*. Get me?"

Neil lost me somewhere around the spelling thing. I didn't get it.

"Look out for yourself and your mission at all costs," Neil continued. "You are the finalists in this exercise. I need some minions, I mean, apprentices to be the brightest and the best. The evilest and the most intelligent, truly proactive evil interns, really, for my next mission." Neil walked among

us, the final six, as he gave this speech. I could feel
Geeky Girl doing her bouncing thing again as he
walked past her. "The winners will be at my side as I
journey into the great unknown." He paused. "That
could be you . . . but only if you win."

"I will win, Mr. Strongarm!" Geeky Girl shouted.

"I think you just might." He nodded at her, and
then walked off. "You have a break now to get some
space food, and then get started on the next task.
Stay in this dome area until you are called to go into
your work zones. Anyone caught out of bounds will
be disqualified. Understand?"

Trevor brought out lots of packets of rehydrated
space food like the astronauts would eat on the
space station. "Better get used to this," he said. "I'm
going to go look for Kirsty and Phillipe. They must
be dealing vith something vith the other campers.
Don't go out of bounds. I'll be back."

We all nodded. I didn't realize how space
competition can make you so hungry. I downed
three packets of space beef stew and rice and some
space ice cream before I went over to speak to Sanj.

"Delighted to be working with you, Mark," he said.

"Really?" I said as I slumped into the chair next to him. "Because I thought you already had a partner for the last couple assessments." I pulled the earpiece from his ear. "Dustin?" I whispered into the earpiece.

"Well, I had some help, yes. Dustin was very helpful accessing the optimal flight path simulation on the NASA database, and looking up the engineering spec for the hand rocket was especially useful, but something's wrong."

"Of course, something is wrong—you cheated," I said.

"No, not that. I mean, Dustin stopped giving me information. I haven't heard from him since the last exercise. That was not the plan, and Dustin is very good at sticking to the plan. Unlike you," he said.

"So, what do you mean? You think he got found out? Or he just stopped?" I said.

"Well, if he was found out, then I wouldn't still be here, would I?" Sanj said. Which was true. "And where are Phillipe and Kirsty? Something is up. But I don't care about all that as much as I care about winning, so the two of us have to trust each other to try to win."

"I don't trust you," I said, getting up. "But I do want to win, so I'll give you one chance. I'll just hold on to this earpiece, so if I find out you are lying to me, I can turn you in as a cheat."

I left Sanj sitting on his own near Bob and Diablo and walked over to Geeky Girl and Igor, who were sitting by the boxes where Fang was hiding. There was a pile of space-food packets nearly as tall as Geeky Girl next to Igor. "Did you try the beef stew?" I said to Igor.

"Urgh!!!" He nodded.

"So, I found out from Sanj that he definitely had help from Dustin for the other tasks, but he says that Dustin stopped talking to him," I said.

"What, Dustin finally got sick of him too?" Geeky Girl said.

"No, he thinks there's something up. Dustin stopped communicating. Kirsty and Phillipe are missing. Maybe something is going on?" I said.

"Sanj is just trying to distract you from whatever his plan is to win," Geeky Girl said, but then paused. "Or maybe now that you're both on the same team, you are trying to distract me and Igor. Yeah, nice try, but I am going to focus on winning this contest and going into space. You can't trick me that easily," she said, and walked off, carrying her helmet with Boris inside.

I sat down next to Igor. "I'm not trying to trick you," I said. "Or Geeky Girl. I don't trust Sanj either, but I don't think he's making this up. Something is going on. Do you want to help me find out what it is?"

Igor nodded and pointed to the corridor that we weren't supposed to go down.

"Yeah, that's what I was thinking too," I said.

We needed a distraction. Fortunately, I

happened to have a very hungry and very bored little furry distraction hiding behind the box we were sitting on.

I drummed lightly on the box with my fingers, and Fang rubbed her head up against my hand. "Fang? Do you want to try the space beef stew?"

Fang purred and licked her sharp, pointy teeth.

Igor picked up Fang, along with a bunch of the empty space-food wrappers, and carried her over to the trash can, which was right behind where Bob and Diablo were sitting.

Diablo had poured his space stew into a bowl and set it down on the floor by his chair. "Hey, man, keep an eye on my food," he said to Bob. "I'm gonna go wash my hands. That Sanj kid said we gotta be really careful with space germs and stuff."

"We're not in space yet . . ." Bob started to say. He was looking through a rocket manual, though, and hardly looked up. "Yeah, sure. Hurry up."

Fang jumped down off the trash can and inhaled all the space stew in seconds flat. She was licking the side of the bowl when Diablo came walking back. She dove behind the trash can.

"Hey, man, you ate my stew! I was saving that!" Diablo pushed Bob.

"I didn't eat your stew," Bob said. "Maybe the wheezy kid ate it?"

"I have a very sensitive stomach. I don't think

that the space stew would agree with me, if you know what I mean," Sanj said.

"Well, someone ate it," Diablo shouted.

And that was the last thing Igor and I heard as we snuck away down the corridor to see what we weren't supposed to see.

11

When Igor and I got to the end of the corridor there was another chamber. This one was taller and slimmer. Silo-shaped with lots of pods all around the edges stacked on top of one another. Walls and walls of these plexiglass pods.

I tapped on one of the pods that sat on the ground. "Empty," I said.

You could see through the plexiglass front. They were clearly made to have someone in them, though. They looked like flat airplane seats encased in plastic.

Igor pointed up. "Urgh?"

"I guess we should check if the others are empty too," I said, so we grabbed a couple of ladders and started climbing.

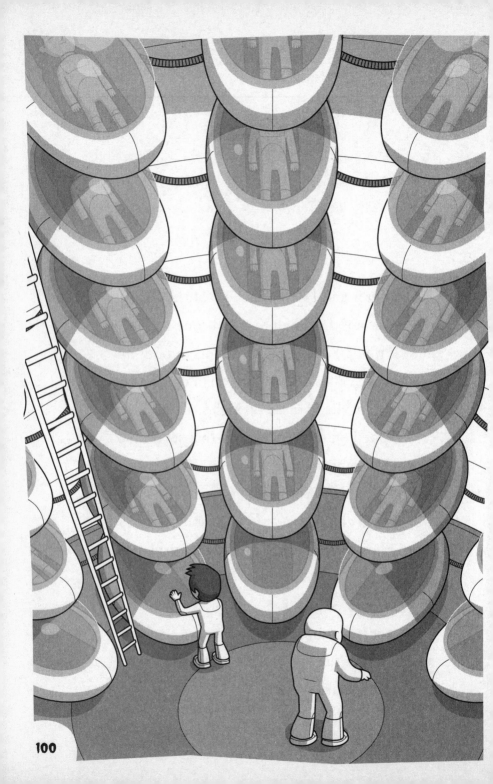

The first couple were empty, and then I spotted one that wasn't. "Igor, that's the Goth girl who was in the last assessment with us!" I looked at the next pod over. "It's the trumpet kid!"

Igor mimed banging on a drum and pointed to the pod near him. "Urgh!"

"The drum kid too?" I said. "But how?"

I tapped on the pod, but they were knocked out or sleeping or something. They were down for the count.

We climbed higher. I started to recognize lots of the kids from camp.

"So, everyone who failed the tests got put into one of these stasis pods instead of being kicked out of the space dome? Maybe they keep them here until the winners are announced and we blast off into space? I guess if our parents signed a form about us going on a space station, they might have said we could all be put in some kind of temporary sleep pods while we're waiting."

"Urgh? Urgh! Urgh!" Igor was pointing to a couple of pods near him.

I slid down my ladder, dragged it over to where his was and climbed up.

"Phillipe? And Kirsty?" I said. "That's weird. Why would they be in a sleep thing? Aren't they running this with Neil Strongarm?"

"Urgh, urgh." Igor pointed to a third pod above them.

"Dustin," I said, looking into the pod, and then shaking it slightly. "And his hair has reverted to its normal bouncy state; look at that."

While we were up the ladder, we heard the door below us open and a motorized gurney with somebody on it wheeled in. There was no one pushing it; it was just on autopilot or something.

The gurney stopped just by an empty pod, and the lid of the pod opened. The gurney then lifted and tilted so the body slid off into the pod. That's when we saw who it was. "Trevor?" I whispered to Igor.

He nodded.

The gurney wheeled back to the door and out again.

We climbed down the ladder and ran over to the pod. Maybe we could wake him before he went completely under. Maybe he could find out what was going on. Besides, if all the camp counselors were sleeping, then there'd be no one to give us the Evil Emperor crowns!

I tapped Trevor's face. "Wake up, Trevor!! We have to try to get you out of here before you end up like the rest of them."

He hardly moved. "You try, Igor," I said.

I moved back and Igor leaned over the pod. He shook Trevor harder, and Trevor opened his eyes a little. He mumbled, "Strongarm."

Then a cloud of gas exploded from the pod. Igor was still leaning over the capsule when it hit.

"Don't breathe in!" I shouted to Igor. "That might be some kind of sleeping gas."

But it was too late. Igor turned to me and mumbled a very sleepy "Urgh" before he collapsed over Trevor's capsule.

"Come on, Igor, just make it to the door. We'll get you some air," I started to say, and then I realized there was no outside air to get him to. Besides, he was already knocked out. I couldn't budge him.

"I'm sorry, Igor," I said.

I snuck out of the pod chamber and back up the corridor. The other kids had stopped fighting about beef stew, and I could see a small gray tail just sticking out from behind the trash can. Fang was safe.

Bob and Diablo were looking over manuals and charts.

Geeky Girl was on her laptop, and Sanj was pacing back and forth with his tablet in his hand.

"You took your time," he whispered as I approached. "Neil Strongarm is about to tell us about our next assessment."

"I hate to tell you when you're right, Sanj, but you were right. There is definitely something up. I found a secret room where everyone is in some sleep-induced stasis," I whispered. "Everyone is stacked up in pods in some suspended-animation silo."

"Everyone from the camp?" he asked. "Dustin? The counselors?"

"Everyone," I said. "It's only us left."

"Interesting," Sanj said.

"Is that all you can say, 'interesting'?!" I whispered a little bit louder. "I tell you that we are all being slowly knocked out and bubbled up, and you say—'INTERESTING'?!"

The last word came out louder than I thought and everyone turned and looked at us.

"Yes, this is an interesting situation, Mark," Sanj responded. "But one that we'll have to deal with after the next stage of the contest."

Sanj paused and looked me right in the eye. "You still want to win, Mark? Do you still want to go into space? Because I do, and I'm doing it with or without you. So I could mention that little gray tail sticking out over there and end this, or I could ask you to sit down and listen to Mr. Strongarm."

Neil Strongarm stepped in front of us. "Everything OK?" he said.

We nodded.

"Are you all ready to start on the next evil phase of your evil journey into space?" Neil asked. Then he looked around. "Hey, where is the big guy?"

Geeky Girl looked around and then looked over at me. "I thought he was with you, Mark," she said.

"Yeah, I saw him in the bathroom down that corridor." I pointed down the way that Igor and I had been when we saw the suspended-animation pods. Neil Strongarm visibly flinched as I pointed in that direction.

"You didn't go down there, did you?" he said with a hint of panic in his voice. "I told you not to leave the area."

12

"We just went to the bathroom," I said, and then I looked over at Geeky Girl. "But Igor wasn't feeling too good. I think maybe he had too much space beef stew and he headed down the corridor, looking for some air, I think."

Geeky Girl shot me a look that I never wanted to see. She knew I was lying, but she thought it was to get Igor in trouble on purpose.

Neil Strongarm looked at Bob. "Well, that is a blow for your team, as it means that the big kid is disqualified for going out of bounds."

"OK, I'll do this challenge on my own then," Bob said.

"I'm sorry. The rules are that if a team member gets disqualified, then the whole team is disqualified," Neil said.

"He can join our team," Diablo said.

"Yes," Geeky Girl agreed. "That only seems fair."

"Why do you think this has to be fair?" Sanj interrupted. "Igor messed up and he's out, and now Bob's out too. I'm sorry, but it means our chances of winning just went up. So actually, I'm not sorry at all."

Neil Strongarm smiled. "The rules stand."

Bob looked over at me and pounded his fist in his hand. "You did this, New Kid. I don't know how, but you set up Igor to go out and get disqualified, and now you've messed up my chances of going into space too."

"It wasn't me," I said, but inside I knew it was. I had asked Igor to go and sneak around with me to see what was going on. If I hadn't, he wouldn't be snoring away now slumped over Trevor's pod and we would all be going forward in the competition.

"Regardless of the circumstances, this means you are out, Bob," Neil said in a don't-mess-with-me voice.

Bob threw his charts down on the ground and stormed off down the corridor. Neil Strongarm followed him.

"I'll be right back," Neil shouted over his shoulder. "Get into your teams and get ready to work."

Neil Strongarm looked over his shoulder at me one more time as he disappeared down the corridor—and he smiled. A smile that said he was proud of me for being so vicious that I got rid of two opponents at once.

As he caught up with Bob at the end of the corridor and closed the door behind him, I knew what he was going to find. He was going to find Igor slumped over Trevor's sleep pod. He was hopefully going to assume that Igor had been alone and snooping and had gotten caught up in the sleeping gas stuff. He would sleep-gas Bob and get him into a pod too, and then there would just be four of us competing to go into space.

I was busy thinking of all these things when Geeky Girl came up and slammed her helmet into my stomach.

"Oooofff!" I said. "What was that for?"

"That was for Igor. I can't believe you would stoop so low as to trick Igor into going out of bounds—and then tell on him! You will stop at nothing to win this, won't you?" she said.

"I didn't trick Igor, and didn't do this on purpose," I said. "Igor was helping me, and something happened."

"Is he OK?" she said.

"He's sleeping," I whispered. "They're all sleeping."

"You're so pathetic. You're trying to distract me with some stupid story so I can't work on my rocket with Diablo. Well, tough luck, because we are not going to be distracted, are we, Diablo?" I'm pretty sure Diablo growled at me then. "And we are going to win anyway," she added. I handed back her helmet with a slightly shaken budgie inside.

"I will keep your one secret, and you keep my one secret," I said to her. "I don't have anything else to hide."

She and Diablo picked up the charts that Bob had dropped and started to look at things on Geeky Girl's laptop.

Sanj strode over to me. "I'm actually impressed, Mark," he said. "That was the evilest thing I think I've seen you do. And I've seen you do lots. To get rid of both Igor and Bob in one evil stroke is genius. We have this contest in the bag now. You and I will be Neil Strongarm's evil protégées in space, and Geeky Girl and Diablo will join the other losers. We just have the slight problem of actually winning the challenge."

Neil Strongarm's footsteps echoed in the corridor

as he approached. This was it. The final challenge. The final four.

"All right then. Four people. Two teams. Two chances to be my right-hand assistants in space." He looked at all of us one by one, and then continued. "Your instructions are in these envelopes. You have to build a rocket that can make it out of the atmosphere and into space. You can use any of the materials in this section."

He handed out the envelopes and then turned before he left down the corridor. "I'll be back in exactly half an hour to test the rockets outside the dome. Better get started." Geeky Girl and Diablo ripped into their envelope and started reading. Sanj was already pulling up diagrams on his tablet and looking at rocket plans.

"I don't get it," I said as I walked over to Sanj. "This seems really easy."

"Maybe Neil Strongarm already knows who he's going to take with him into space and this is simply a formality. We just have to make something that works, and we'll win," Sanj said.

"I don't trust him," I said, "but I don't trust you either. So we're going to work on this rocket thing together so I can make sure you're not going to double-cross me at the last minute. Agreed?"

"Agreed," Sanj said.

Geeky Girl glared at me from across the room as she and Diablo started taking apart bits of equipment in the dome to make their rocket.

We worked fast. We were all good at what we were doing, and there was plenty of equipment to cannibalize. There were so many quality parts in there, I got a bit bored and started playing with stuff for my inventions. I pulled my prototype mini lunar pogo stick out of my sock and worked up a cool turbo boost for the base.

"Do you think this megaspring is long enough to bounce a pogo stick in zero gravity?" I asked Sanj.

"Only you could be bored in the middle of a rocket-making space race," Sanj said. "Put that down and finish the control panel."

"OK, fine," I moaned. I put the mini lunar pogo stick up my pants leg and into my sock for safekeeping, then I attached the last few buttons and switches to the panel.

In only fifteen minutes we had put together a small, efficient rocket that could get into space.

"That's it. It's done," I said as I connected the last few wires of our rocket.

"Marvelous," Sanj said, standing back and looking at our creation. "Nearly perfect. I might want to make a small adaptation. Why don't you use your evil skills and see if you can eliminate any of our opponents?"

I looked over at Geeky Girl and Diablo. They looked done too. Diablo was just adding some design bits to the sides of the rocket—metal twists that looked like flames shooting out. Geeky Girl left him to it and sat down to look at something on her laptop.

I nodded to Sanj. "I'll see what I can do." I walked up to Geeky Girl. On my way I passed Fang and whispered, "Keep an eye on Sanj, kitten. I still don't trust that he's not gonna double-cross us."

She purred, licked her paw and skulked over to crouch behind a bench near Sanj. That was a yes, then, I guess. I continued over to Geeky Girl.

I motioned for her to come over to where I was standing by the entrance to the corridor. She rolled her eyes and stomped over to where I was waiting, out of earshot of the others.

"Well?" she huffed.

"Aren't you curious?" I asked her. "What Igor and I found? Why Strongarm gave us such an easy final task (which I'm totally going to win, by the way)? Don't you want to know what's really going on?"

13

She glared at me.

I said it again: "Something is wrong. Don't you want to know what?"

"Look, Diablo and I are going to win this. Our rocket is perfect." She paused. "Something is wrong here, but I already know what it is." She paused again and glared at me. "It's you."

"Look, you have to believe me. They're all trapped in these suspended-animation pods. We saw them. Trevor, Kirsty and Phillipe are all down there. The trumpet kid is in a row on the side and the drumming kid is below him. Dustin is in there too, and you know his hair still shakes back into place even in suspended animation?"

"You checked?" she said.

"Kinda," I answered.

"And you want me to believe that Igor is in there too?" she said.

"Yes! We came across the pod place, but then we saw that they were just about to gas Trevor to sleep, and Igor was leaning over the capsule, and he got gassed too," I explained.

"Sure, that all makes perfect sense. So Strongarm set up this whole series of space tests just so he could trap a bunch of kids from a camp in sleep pods?" she said. "Is that what you told Igor to get him to follow you out of bounds?"

"No, we didn't know about the pods until we saw them—" I started, but Geeky Girl interrupted.

"You can stop lying now, Mark. It's not going to work with me. I'm not following you anywhere," she said.

"But . . ." I said.

"I'm getting back to work." She turned and headed back to Diablo.

How could she not believe me? Then I thought about it. Nothing I had told her made any sense. I mean, I almost didn't believe it myself. Why would she buy it? And especially why would she believe it from me after she thought I betrayed Igor?

Nope, I was on my own.

"Every person for themselves." Isn't that what Geeky Girl said right after she blasted me in the race?

If there was nothing I could do about this weird space pod stuff, then I'd get my mind back to winning this contest. One hundred percent commitment. To quote Neil Strongarm, "You're either in the rocket or on the ground. There's no halfway in space."

I was going to show Neil Strongarm that I was the best evil space assistant on the planet—heck, in the universe—and he would be crazy not to pick me.

I walked back over to where they were all working. Geeky Girl was holding their shiny red rocket while Diablo put the final touches on the decoration. It had a fireball painted on the side and metal strips that had been shaped and twisted to look like silver flames coming out of it. I had to admit it looked cool . . . or hot . . . It looked good.

"I call her Fuego!!" Diablo said proudly as he wiped a smudge off the side of the rocket.

Sanj was tapping away at some buttons on the side of our rocket.

"Good, you're back," Sanj said. "Oh"—he paused—"she's still with you. Well, we'll just have to let our rocket win then after all."

At that moment, Neil Strongarm walked into the room.

"Good. It looks like we are ready to launch the final stage of this contest. Why don't you all join me outside and we can test the rockets." He looked around at each of us. "This is the final countdown, people. Let's see what you can do."

Diablo carried out their rocket and Geeky Girl held her helmet with Boris tucked inside. Sanj picked up our rocket right away and started toward the dome entrance.

"I can't wait to breathe some fresh air," I said.

"I prefer the air in the dome. Better for my sinuses," Sanj said.

As I headed out, I looked around the trash can for Fang, but she wasn't there. "Sanj, have you seen Fang?" I whispered as we got outside.

"Oh . . . yes . . . I saw her dash outside behind Neil Strongarm as soon as he opened the door. But don't worry, no one else did," he said. "Come on. We can't keep Neil Strongarm waiting."

That totally sounded like what Fang would do. She wouldn't want to stay in that dome a second longer than she had to. She was probably out here enjoying herself, climbing an actual tree or picking a fight with a squirrel.

As we put our rockets on the launch pads outside, it occurred to me for the first time—what if Fang didn't want to come with me into space? My thinking was interrupted by a popping sound. We looked back and the dome had started to deflate. It was getting sucked back into the capsules that it had come out of, which was impressive. But the big rocket-shaped silo it revealed as it deflated was even more impressive.

Then two gigantic arms sprang out from the silo and extended. Drapes of material unfurled into two huge, powerful wings.

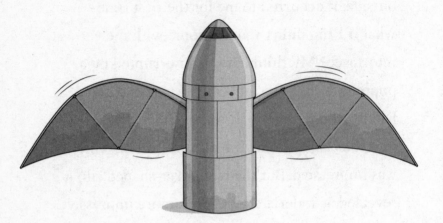

"He stole my idea!" Geeky Girl said. "The WOOSSH technology! Winged Onboard Oscillating Solar Sail Hybrids! He stole it!"

At that moment, Neil Strongarm stepped out from behind the silo and walked toward us. "All's fair in space and war," he said, grinning. "So now you see the culmination of my plans. Here is what it was all for. Oh, and thanks for the wing idea too, kid," he added, and winked. "This is your chance to show me that you could be my evil apprentices on my journey into space. Launch your rockets into space now and my giant space ark will follow!"

"Wait, do you mean *ark* as in two by two and Noah and animals and stuff?" I asked. "Because I might have changed my mind about space if it's going to be filled with bears and raccoons too."

Neil Strongarm laughed a really full-belly laugh like an evil Santa Claus. "I can promise you, there are no animals on my ark. It has only human passengers."

"Not really sure what you mean with all that ark stuff, but we are ready to rocket!" Diablo said.

Geeky Girl caught my eye and mouthed the words, "Is the ark full of the space pods?"

I nodded.

"Is Igor on that ark?" she mouthed again.

I nodded a second time.

Geeky Girl walked up to the launch pad and put the helmet down by her feet. Then Diablo strode up and patted the rocket on the side. "Fly well, Fuego," he said.

Diablo leaned over and set the launch sequence.

"Ten, nine, eight, seven, six"—the countdown was on—"five, four, three . . ."

Then Geeky Girl got a glint in her eye and slightly tapped the helmet on the ground with her foot.

"Two . . ."

Boris flapped up into the air and flew right into Diablo, who stumbled back into the rocket, knocking it off center.

"One." The rocket launched.

"Nooo!" Diablo shouted as he scrambled to his feet and Boris flew up into a nearby tree.

"That's heading right for ..." Neil Strongarm stared at his winged ark in disbelief.

The rocket shot into the air and tore a hole through the sail on the left side of the rocket. Then it continued up into the atmosphere and out of sight.

"That is unfortunate," Neil Strongarm said, shaking his head.

Geeky Girl stopped herself from smiling and put on a look of shock. She was a better actor than I thought.

Neil stepped toward Diablo and Geeky Girl. "There are no second chances in space," Neil said as he pulled out a spray can from his bag. The label on the side said:

QUICK-ACTING
**EVIL SCIENTIST
SLEEP SPRAY**
(SUPER-DROWSY
FORMULA)

He turned toward Diablo and sprayed. "What? Man . . . why am I feeling so . . . zzzzzzzz." Diablo was snoring in seconds.

"Did you have to—" Geeky Girl started to say, but Neil interrupted.

"Yes, mistakes can't happen in space. But lucky for you, that just increased your chances of winning. You should be pleased," he said.

"I am definitely pleased," Sanj said, and wheezed a feeble "Mwhaa-haa-haa-haa."

I looked down at Diablo, knocked out by the sleeping gas, and then up at the big rocket ship with all the campers inside and the left sail dangling loosely from the side.

"Yeah, great news about the winning and all, but don't you think it's kind of a big problem that there's a massive hole in your sail now?" I said.

"You see, that would be a problem, if a clever young evil apprentice hadn't come up with an Evil Super Space-Expanding Foam," he said. "I've made some modifications, so it works well on fabric now too."

Strongarm opened a briefcase with a control panel inside. He pressed some buttons and a little robot flew out of the silo with what looked like a fire extinguisher. He sprayed the hole and the expanding foam blocked it up perfectly.

"See." Strongarm smiled. "I knew you would be useful to have along for the ride." He paused. "In fact, I've just decided that you, Mark, have won a place as my evil space apprentice."

My mind was in full-throttle spin. I was going

into space with Neil Strongarm! The only problem was that it looked like Neil was kidnapping the whole camp to take with us.

Neil looked down at Geeky Girl and Sanj. "The two of you will have to convince me which of you is most worthy to get the other place."

Geeky Girl spoke up right away. "Can I just say that you wouldn't have wings on that ark in the first place if it wasn't for my idea that you stole . . . I mean, borrowed?" she added.

"Please. We are evil. We don't borrow, we steal." He laughed. "I stole your idea and I made it better. Like I did with Mark's. It's what I do. It's my own form of evil genius."

Sanj interrupted, "Mr. Strongarm, speaking as one evil genius to another, I think I can prove to you that I will be even more useful as an evil space assistant by showing you my ingenious upgrade to our rocket. Besides, Mark and I have worked together on so many evil plans over the years, you would be getting a ready-made team of evil apprentices if you take us both."

Neil Strongarm looked back and forth between them and then declared, "I have the perfect way to decide." He turned to me and held out his hand, clutching the can of Quick-Acting Evil Scientist Sleep Spray.

"You choose, Mark," Neil said, and handed me the spray. "The loser gets a long sleep and the winner gets to join you at my side. Simple and evil."

I took the spray and stared over at Sanj and Geeky Girl. "I choose?"

"We're so close, Mark," he said, putting his one hand on my shoulder and pointing into the sky with the other. I seriously thought that if evil people in the future ever made a statue of me and Neil Strongarm to mark this moment when the evil exploration of space started, this would be the pose on the statue. And it would be epic.

"All the years of planning. All the countless talk shows, books and interviews where I had to talk about space travel when what I really wanted was to start my own evil planet with an evil space station on it filled with all my evil minions. And now I can!" Neil laughed a pretty impressive *mwhaaa-haa-haaa-haa* laugh, and ended it with, "You are lucky that you are going to be a part of it. You can help write evil history. To evilly go where no one has gone before!"

"I hate to interrupt when you are busy misquoting *Star Trek* and all, but ..." Geeky Girl turned to me. "Who are you going to pick?" She looked me right in the eye.

"I think you know what you have to do, Mark,"
Sanj said. "My evil best friend."

I took the spray and strode up to Geeky Girl.
When I was blocking Neil Strongarm's view of
her face, she nodded slightly and winked. "Do it.
Quick," she mouthed. She closed her eyes and held
her breath. I pointed the can toward her face so
Strongarm could see and sprayed.

Geeky Girl collapsed at my feet. Boris flew down from the tree and perched on her shoulder, gently nudging her with his beak to try to wake her. I shooed him away with my hand. "Get outta here, you random bird that's not connected to Geeky Girl in any way."

"What are you mumbling, Mark?" Strongarm asked.

"Nothing," I said.

"So, good decision, Mark," Strongarm said. I handed him back the spray can while Sanj stood by our rocket on the launch pad, holding it steady so it didn't fall over.

Neil stepped out in front of the launch pad. "So, you two are my evil space apprentices," he said, looking us up and down. "I guess I can live with that. We can fly off into space and you can both help me rule my new evil space station with all the campers and counselors as my minions."

He broke out into a loud "Mwhaaa-haa-haa-haa."

Sanj joined in with his own wheezy version of his laugh, and I could feel a deep *mwhaa-haa-haa-haa* welling up inside me. This was what I had dreamed of. I'd be an evil ruler. I could boss around Trevor, Phillipe and Kirsty, and most definitely Bob and Diablo and Dustin. I could even get someone to make me a proper crown for my space helmet. But I wasn't laughing. I was thinking about Igor and Geeky Girl, and I was thinking about Fang. She would HATE space. Why was I doing this?

Then it hit me. Sometimes thoughts sneak up on you like a super-sly ninja with ultimate stealth powers. This was one of those thoughts. *Where was Fang?*

"We still need to launch our rocket into space," Sanj said when he got his breath back from the *mwhaa-haa-haa*ing. "Like your rocket there, I have modified ours so that it can carry passengers . . . well, one small passenger." Sanj laughed his evil wheeze. "Mwahhh-haaa-haa haa-eaaaazzz."

I ran over to the rocket and saw a gray paw clawing at the hatch!

"Fang!" I shouted, and pounded on the hatch. "You put Fang in the rocket, Sanj!"

"I had to see if my life-support system would work, and I'm certainly not going to try it out on myself," he said.

"Get her out of there!" I pulled at the hatch door, trying to find the release switch.

"Why do you care about a stupid cat?" Neil Strongarm sneered. "Is it yours?" He paused. "Well, you wouldn't be able to take it into space anyway, so you might as well let Sanj here use it to further the cause of science."

"I'll use you to further the cause of science if you don't shut up about my kitten," I shouted at Strongarm. I stepped toward Sanj. "Now, let her out now!"

"No time. The launch is starting," Sanj said, and stepped away from the launch pad.

I had to get Fang out of there.

The countdown started. "Ten, nine, eight, seven, six . . ."

15

I looked around for anything that I could use to jam open the hatch and get Fang out of there.

Then I saw Geeky Girl move on the ground. "Boris!" she shouted. "The rocket hatch! Hurry!"

"Five . . . four . . ."

"That bird won't be able to smash the glass. It's meteor proof." Sanj laughed.

Boris flapped over and slipped his claws into the latch of the rocket door, like he was picking a lock.

"Three, two . . ."

"CLICK!" The lock turned, and the hatch pinged open.

"One."

Boris flew back to Geeky Girl's side. Fang leaped out of the rocket into my arms, and I dove out of the way as the rocket ignited and took off!

The rocket whooshed up into the sky, but then it wobbled, probably because the hatch was blowing back and forth in the wind. It veered off and crashed down to the ground in a ball of fire.

"Noooo!" Sanj whined.

I ran over to Geeky Girl and Boris with Fang squirming under my arm.

"Are you OK?" I whispered.

Geeky Girl sat up. "Yes, I'm fine. I used to free dive in Tahiti. I can hold my breath for like five minutes straight."

"Cool," I said.

"As touching as this little reunion and cat rescue are, I'm afraid I'm going to have to stop you there," Neil Strongarm interrupted. "You've just given up the opportunity of a lifetime, Mark. I can't take you into space now."

"I think I changed my mind about wanting to go into space anyway," I said. "And I think we're going to stop you from taking everyone else into space too."

Neil laughed a powerful "Mwhaa-haa-haa-haa."

"You can't stop me," he said. "Now that I have the super-expanding space foam, I can fix any hole you manage to put in the space sails. I will blast off and take the whole camp with me, and there's nothing you can do about it."

"Yeah, so there," Sanj added.

"It's a shame it has to end like this, Mark," Strongarm said as he took the cap off the sleep spray and started walking toward Geeky Girl and me. "I thought you would make a fine space apprentice, but you tricked me about spraying the girl and you sabotaged the rocket just to rescue a stupid kitten," he continued.

"I think you are going to have to stop calling Fang a stupid kitten if you don't want to get shredded," I said.

Then I looked down at Fang, who was still squirming and itching for a fight.

"Yeah, shredded," I said, and smiled at Geeky Girl.

"Shredded. As in, not able to be repaired by any space-foam stuff? Hmmmm?" she said. "I think we might know someone who could do that."

I bolted with Fang toward the WOOSSH sails and shouted to Neil as I stood below the sails, "Hey, change of plans. How about instead of you gassing us and taking us up into space as your minions, we stop you from launching the whole camp into space instead."

Strongarm was between me and Geeky Girl. He could spray only one of us at a time, and all I needed was a moment to get away. Geeky Girl knew just what to do.

"Oh, and Neil," Geeky Girl shouted, "Neil Armstrong was a way better astronaut. That's why they sent him to the moon first."

Neil Strongarm turned Fuego Rocket red, lurched toward Geeky Girl and sprayed.

BOING!

In that second, I pulled the mini lunar pogo stick out from my sock and bounced. "Hang on, Fang!" I yelled. That pogo stick had some spring in it. We were up over the top of the sails in a second. Fang waited until the pogo stick had sailed past the right wing before she jumped. Her claws caught the side of the wing and dug in. Eighteen kitty-cat blades of destruction cut into the wing. The sound of fabric shredding filled the air.

"My beautiful wings!" Neil Strongarm yelled.

Fang was sliding down the sail with her claws out, slicing the fabric as she slid.

"Get off my space wings," Neil Strongarm yelled as he grabbed the bottom corner of the material and flicked it. The wobble went up the material until it hit Fang and shook her clean off the sail.

I landed with the pogo stick and bounced up again. "I got you, Fang!" I shouted.

"Not this time," Sanj shouted as he threw his backpack toward me. It knocked into the stick and sent me falling.

"Oooof!" I hit the ground with a thud. "Fang," I mumbled, looking up at the sky.

She was crashing down on the other side of the silo. There was no way I could get there. "Fang!"

Then I saw a flash of green and yellow streak past me. Boris flew up and caught Fang's fur in her claws. He wobbled under the weight of the kitten, but he staggered down to land by the launch pad. They tumbled to a halt just by where the rocket had taken off. I scooped up Fang in my arms. "You did it, Fang! Those wings are toast! Who's my evil kitteny whitteny?" I squished her in a bear hug as strong as Igor could. Which reminded me . . .

"Igor?!" I shouted. "We've got to get him out. And the others."

Geeky Girl was already at the rocket silo. "I'm on it!" she shouted back. "I think I can override the commands on the control panel."

As Fang wriggled free, she jumped down into a natural attack stance.

Neil Strongarm was headed toward us and he did not look happy.

16

"You've ruined everything!" he said. "My beautiful wings on my beautiful spaceship!"

"Yeah, sorry, did we ruin your plan to kidnap the whole Evil Scientist Summer Camp and take us off to some stupid planet to be your space minions? Boohoo," I said.

Then I saw he had a box in his hand. One of those boxes with a big red button on it. The kind that you don't want to see get pressed.

"This is the self-destruct button for the rocket. If I can't launch my rocket, then I'll blow the whole thing up here." Neil Strongarm was ranting now.

"I'll do it too. I'll—" But Neil Strongarm didn't get to finish his threat. A helmet, held by a very sleepy-looking Igor, came down on his head, and Strongarm stopped talking and started snoring pretty fast.

"Igor!" I said. "Hey, are you OK, man?"

"Urgh, urgh, urgh." He grunted and rubbed his eyes. Fang curled around Igor's legs. "Urghhhhh." He scratched her behind the ear.

Then Trevor emerged from the silo, yawning and stretching. Followed by Kirsty, Phillipe and some of the missing kids.

"Time for you pets to hide again," I whispered to Fang and Boris. "No sense in saving us all from being shot into space just to end up sent home in the Canoe of Shame instead."

Fang jumped and Boris fluttered into Igor's space helmet. I picked it up and tucked it under my arm.

Trevor, Kirsty and Phillipe walked onto the launch pad and looked around. They saw Sanj still bent over our rocket, whining, saying how it would have been perfect if I hadn't messed it up.

Igor grabbed another spray can from Neil's bag that said SUPER EVIL SLEEP SPRAY ANTIDOTE, and walked over to Diablo. One spray and he was mumbling. . . .

"Hey, that Strongarm guy went a bit loco," he said, and yawned. "How did I get here?"

"Urgh," Igor answered as he helped Diablo stand up.

Soon the others started coming out of the silo too: Bob, Dustin and more kids.

I was standing triumphantly over the snoring body of Neil Strongarm, with the pets tucked away in the helmet under my arm, and I was smiling. It gave me an idea for an even better statue.

SNORE!

Everyone else in the camp was wandering around outside, looking confused and very tired.

"So, who is going to explain what happened?" Kirsty finally said.

"Ummmm, that would be me," Geeky Girl shouted from over by the rocket-silo door. "I think that's the last of the pods released, but let me know if you think anyone else is still missing."

She walked up onto the launch pad and stepped over Neil Strongarm.

"Do you want the long or the short version?" she asked.

Trevor, Phillipe and Kirsty looked at one another. "The short version," Trevor said.

"So, Neil Strongarm had this ultra-secret plan to knock out everyone in the camp, put you into suspended-animation pods and then blast you off to build a space station for him on a new planet, and you would be like his space-minion slaves."

"What? The last thing I remember, I was giving Strongarm the results of the harness assessment, and then I woke up in that pod thing," Kirsty said.

"Mark figured it out," Geeky Girl said.

"Urgh," Igor added.

"And Igor," I said, "but he got sleep-gassed, and there were only a couple of us left to try to defeat Strongarm's plan."

The counselors looked down at Strongarm lying on the floor. "Urgh." Igor demonstrated the hit with the helmet.

"Ahhh." Phillipe nodded.

"That wasn't actually part of the plan, but it was an epic ad-lib by Igor," I said, and high-fived Igor too.

"So what happens now?" Geeky Girl said. "Now that we've caught Neil Strongarm and foiled his plan, do we call, like, the space police or something to come and get him?"

Every camper in the place stopped and stared at Geeky Girl. It was like she had just said the name of Neil Strongarm's space station, SSSH.

"We don't call zee police," Phillipe said, shaking his head. "Are you sure you are really a young EVIL scientist?"

"Haaa-haaa-haa-haaa." I started to laugh really loudly and patted Igor on the back to get him to laugh too. "Mwhaa-haa-haa! Good one! Space police!" I said.

Igor and some of the other kids joined in too.

"Oh, it's a little joke to lighten zee mood, I see," Phillipe said. "Of course we wouldn't call zee police. Being evil and all." He giggled. "Zat's a good one."

"Ve vill have to call the Bureau for Evil Double-Crossing, though," Trevor interrupted. "There are rules that Strongarm broke, and he'll have to pay the fine."

Trevor and Igor went and got one of the empty pods and put Strongarm inside.

Then Kirsty wrote "Please deliver to . . ." and the address of the Bureau of Evil Double-Crossing on the front in paint with the note of who was inside.

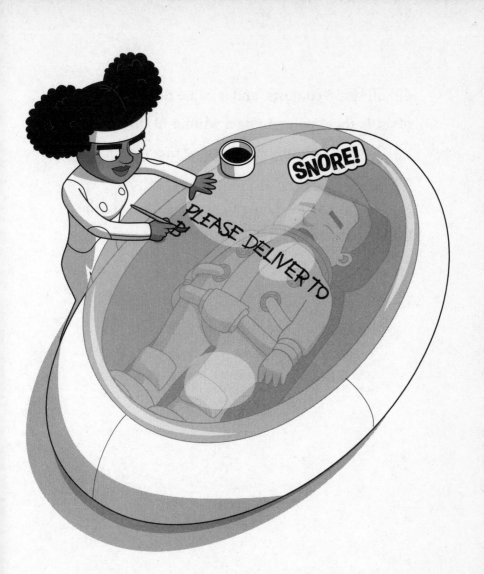

"Excuse me?" Geeky Girl tapped Trevor on the leg as he was closing the hatch on Strongarm's space pod. "I get it that no one is going into space. And I'm pretty OK with that now, actually. But we did all those contests, and it came down to the four of us. Is there going to be a winner of the week?"

"Yeah, who's Evil Emperor of the Week?" I asked.

"And is anyone going to get sent home in the Canoe of Shame?" Bob said.

17

"I should be Evil Emperor, of course," Sanj said. "I scored the highest on all the tests and I designed the best rocket in the final one."

"Where is that rocket now?" Kirsty asked Sanj.

Sanj looked down at the burned-out ball of metal at his feet that used to be the rocket.

"No, you don't win then," Kirsty said.

"Well, Mark and Igor and I saved the whole camp from being blasted off into space," Geeky Girl said.

"The title of the prize is EVIL Emperor of the Week, and you expect us to give it to you for doing something nice?" Kirsty stared Geeky Girl down.

"I guess not," Geeky Girl said.

"Vat happened to your rocket?" Trevor asked me.

"Um, Sanj and I had the same rocket, so it kind of crashed." I gulped.

"You don't win then."

"Diablo and my rocket flew into the wing and tore a big hole in it before it then headed up into the sky," Geeky Girl admitted.

"I didn't really see where it went because I got sprayed with sleep gas," Diablo added.

"Sleep gas?" Trevor asked.

"Yeah, this," I said, holding up the can. "Kinda cool invention. Not as cool as Evil Super Space-Expanding Foam or a Pogo Stick Lunar Travel Individual Vehicle, but kinda cool."

"So your rocket completed zee task and made it into space?" Phillipe asked.

"We might not be in space, but Fuego is!" Diablo pointed up to the sky.

"Then you are Evil Emperor of the Week, Diablo. Geeky Girl is disqualified for nice behavior," Kirsty said. "Not sure where the certificates are, though . . ." she added.

"So, who is going home?" Bob said, glaring at me. "I have an idea who it should be. What do you think, New Kid?"

"Umm. Yeah . . . I have an idea," I said, and walked over and took the paintbrush from the pot where Kirsty had left it. I dipped it into the black paint and wrote POD OF SHAME on the side of the space pod with Strongarm inside.

The counselors looked at one another. "Agreed," they said.

Trevor and Igor carried the pod down to the river, and we all followed. They held the pod over the water's edge. Strongarm was awake now and banging on the inside, demanding to be let out.

"Don't worry," said Kirsty, pressing the
microphone link on the pod so Neil could hear
what was said outside, "someone will return you to
the bureau soon enough. In the meantime, enjoy
the scenery."

Geeky Girl smiled and added, "Yeah, and
remember, it's really only one small splash for man,
one massive splash for all mankind."

Neil Strongarm bashed against the inside of the pod, turning that Fuego red all over again.

The pod splashed down into the river and floated downstream toward town.

We all wandered back to our tents. Almost everyone else was still sleepy from the artificial suspended animation. Geeky Girl, Sanj and I were all wide-awake.

Bob rubbed his eyes as he and Diablo pushed past us on the way to the tent. "You might be safe this week, New Kid, but next time you'll be outta here," Bob said, and sneezed. "You made me lose that contest. I could have been up in space now if it wasn't for you." He mumbled as he and Diablo stomped off.

"Yeah, you would be up in space now . . . as an evil minion!" I shouted back. "No need to say thanks for saving you or anything."

Sanj tapped me on the shoulder.

"You think you and your stupid cat can stomp on my space dreams and get away with it?"

Fang pounced toward Sanj with claws out.

"OOOOWWWW!" Sanj yelped.

"You really should know by now not to call Fang stupid." I shook my head.

"That's it! I'm finding the counselors right now to tell them about your stup—"

He paused as Fang growled at him.

"About your . . . cat and the budgie." Sanj folded his arms. "There's a canoe with your name on it. Well, all your names on it. Or two canoes. I don't know. All I know is you'll be gone," he huffed.

Fang jumped onto my lap, and I stroked her until she stopped growling at Sanj.

"Actually, Sanj," I said, "I don't think you're gonna tell." I smiled. "You see, I still have the earpiece that you used to cheat with Dustin on the tests. You and Dustin could still end up sharing a Canoe of Shame on the way home if we tell on you."

"Checkmate," Sanj said. "But just for this game." He stomped off toward his tent.

Geeky Girl, Igor and I all lay down on the grass outside the tent and looked up at the sky. The sun was going down and the stars were coming out.

"I remember going to my grandma's house in Tahiti when I was really, really young," Geeky Girl said. "I used to stand on the balcony and look up at the stars. The stars there are nothing like the ones we see back home."

"Um, hate to say. Kinda basic fact here," I whispered. "Yeah, they are definitely the same stars."

"I mean they don't look anywhere near the same. There are soooo many of them, and there's no light from towns or cities out where my grandma lives. It's so dark that you actually see every star. I used to say that I would get out there into space one day and be an astronaut."

"Did you ever have a Neil Strongarm action figure?" I asked Geeky Girl.

"No!" she said.

"Did you shoot your dolls up in rockets or anything?" I asked. "Just wondering? No reason."

"I didn't play with dolls, really, but if I did, I don't think I would have shot them into space, no. I studied about space. Watched TV shows and videos, read anything I could about it." She paused and rocked Boris in his helmet like it was a little budgie cradle or something. "Boris is named after a cosmonaut, you know."

"Urgh." Igor nodded.

"Cool," I said.

"Do you wish you were up in space?" I asked Igor.

Igor shook his head. "Urgh, urgh, urgh!"

"No, I guess being locked up in a space-pod thing would kinda put you off, huh," I agreed.

"I will be in space someday," Geeky Girl said. "But not as a minion slave to some egomaniacal evil astronaut. I'll get there. Just not today."

"Yeah, I don't know why I spent so much time thinking I wanted to be like that guy," I said. "You know, his action figure didn't even fly that well," I added.

"Urgh," Igor agreed.

"I did like the space food, though, way better than the normal camp food. Shame that's all lost with the dome," I said.

"Urgh, urgh?" Igor looked a bit guilty and then unzipped his backpack. Packets and packets of space beef stew and space ice cream tumbled out.

"Dinner!" I said, high-fiving Igor and tossing a packet of ice cream to Geeky Girl.

"Hey, Fang." I peered into the space helmet where she was hiding to see if she wanted some beef stew for her dinner. "Oh, look," I said.

Fang was curled up in a ball in the helmet fast asleep, with Boris perched on her tail, snoozing.

"I guess they had a long day," Geeky Girl said.

Dear Mom,

I actually learned something this week in camp.

Well, I learned a couple things.

I learned that there is no _I_ in team, but there is an _I_ in survival.

I learned that there is totally a <u>cat</u> in <u>catastrophe</u>, but there is no trophy at the end of it, and there's definitely not a crown. What does a guy have to do around here to get a crown?

I learned you can't play marbles in space, but sometimes space can make you lose your marbles.

And space ice cream is pretty epic.

Tell Sami I'll sneak some home for her.

Your son,
Mark

P.S. You can totally throw away my Neil Strongarm action figure. It's under the bed.

ACKNOWLEDGMENTS

Most of this book was written with a kitten curled up on my lap (or on my laptop), so this is dedicated to all the furry friends in my life (vampire or otherwise).

Mark is doing okay against Evil Scientist Summer Camp,
but annoying little brothers are a different story....

For more FIN-TASTICALLY FISHY mayhem, check out:

ZOMBIEGOLDFISHBOOKS.COM

Thank you for reading this Feiwel and Friends book.
The Friends who made

My FANGtastically Evil Vampire Pet

possible are:

Jean Feiwel	Liz Szabla
PUBLISHER	**ASSOCIATE PUBLISHER**
Rich Deas	Holly West
SENIOR CREATIVE DIRECTOR	**EDITOR**
Alexei Esikoff	Kim Waymer
SENIOR MANAGING EDITOR	**SENIOR PRODUCTION MANAGER**
Anna Roberto	Val Otarod
EDITOR	**ASSOCIATE EDITOR**
Kat Brzozowski	Anna Poon
EDITOR	**ASSISTANT EDITOR**
Emily Settle	Carol Ly
ASSISTANT EDITOR	**DESIGNER**

**Follow us on Facebook or
visit us online at mackids.com.**

Our Books are Friends for Life